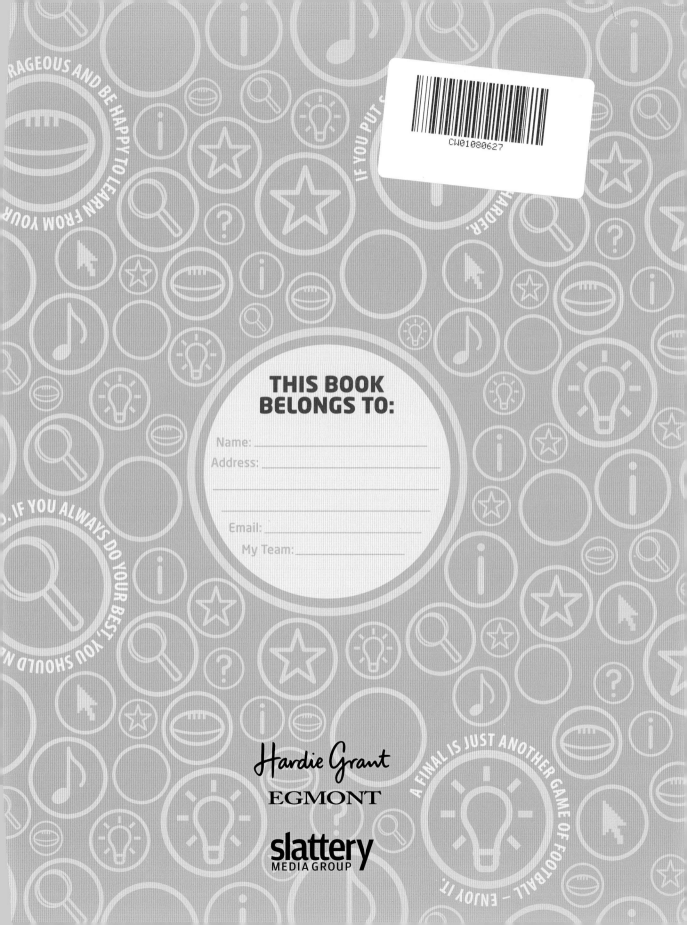

RAGEOUS AND BE HAPPY TO LEARN FROM YOUR

IF YOU PUT ...

...ARDER.

IF YOU ALWAYS DO YOUR BEST, YOU SHOULD N...

A FINAL IS JUST ANOTHER GAME OF FOOTBALL – ENJOY IT.

**THIS BOOK BELONGS TO:**

Name: _____

Address: _____

_____

_____

Email: _____

My Team: _____

*Hardie Grant*

EGMONT

**slattery**
MEDIA GROUP

*Fabulous Fantastic Footy Fun & Fact Book*
published in 2020 by
Hardie Grant Egmont
Ground Floor, Building 1, 658 Church Street
Richmond, Victoria 3121, Australia
www.hardiegrantegmont.com

Produced in 2020 by
The Slattery Media Group

Parts of this book were first published in 2005 as

*Dipper's Fabulous Fantastic Footy Fun (& Fact) Book*
by The Slattery Media Group
(2005 design: Andrew Hutchison)

Photos by AFL Photos (aflphotos.com.au) and used with the permission of the Australian Football League, AFL House, 140 Harbour Esplanade, Docklands, Victoria, Australia, 3008.

Unsplash images: pages 100, 108, 109.
Cover images: AFL Mascots

A catalogue record for this book is available from the National Library of Australia

Text copyright © The Slattery Media Group 2020
Publication copyright © Hardie Grant Egmont 2020

Publisher: Geoff Slattery
Art Director and designer: Kate Slattery

Content by: Kevan Carroll, Ben Collins, Ben Cuthbertson, Peter DiSisto, Russell Jackson, Michael Lovett, Jim Main, John Murray, Geoff Slattery, Janelle Ward.

ISBN: 9781760504182

Printed in China by Leo Paper Group.

1 3 5 7 9 10 8 6 4 2

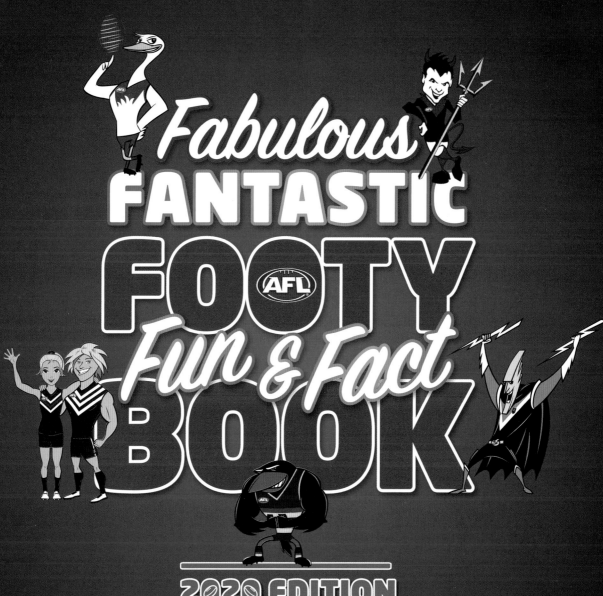

# Fabulous FANTASTIC FOOTY Fun & Fact BOOK

## 2020 EDITION

# DEAR FOOTY FAN,

This book aims to challenge, entertain and inform, but most of all, it's meant to be FUN.

You will learn about all the clubs, the record-breakers, the quirky and the UNBELIEVABLE. You'll find puzzles, history, trivia, and some wisdom from the greats of the game; there are even some healthy recipes to make your day at the footy just a little more enjoyable. The puzzles are not all easy: some of them might even baffle mums and dads and grandparents—even AFL stars!

## HAVE FUN!

# CONTENTS

Statistics accurate to the end of the 2019 AFL and 2019 AFLW seasons. At the time of publication, not all Club captains had been announced for the 2020 Toyota AFL Premiership Season.

**DEGREE OF DIFFICULTY**

★☆☆ EASY (SUIT 7+)
★★☆ MEDIUM (SUIT 8+)
★★★ HARD (SUIT 10+)

**ALL ABOUT...** YOU

# PERSONAL DETAILS...

NAME: .................................................................
.................................................................

NICKNAME: ...........................................................

BORN: ............/............/............

SCHOOL: .............................................................
.................................................................

HOBBIES: ............................................................
.................................................................

WHEN YOU GROW UP, YOU WANT TO BE A:
.................................................................

FAVOURITE BOOK: ....................................................
.................................................................

FAVOURITE TV SHOW: .................................................

FAVOURITE SONG: ....................................................

INSTAGRAM HANDLE: ..................................................

# JUNIOR FOOTY

AFL AUSKICK CENTRE/JUNIOR FOOTY CLUB:
.................................................................
.................................................................

CLUB COLOURS: ......................................................

CLUB NICKNAME: .....................................................

CLUB MOTTO: ........................................................

JUMPER NUMBER: .....................................................

POSITIONS PLAYED: ..................................................

BEST FOOTY MOMENT SO FAR: ..........................................
.................................................................
.................................................................

FOOTY DREAM: .......................................................
.................................................................
.................................................................

SKILLS YOU NEED TO PRACTISE: .......................................
.................................................................

# AFL FOOTY

**YOUR FAVOURITE AFL CLUB:** ............................................................................................

**Why:** ..............................................................................................................................

**WHEN YOU STARTED BARRACKING FOR THEM:** ..............................................................

**CLUB NICKNAME:** ...........................................................................................................

**CLUB MASCOT:** ...............................................................................................................

**HOME GROUND:** .............................................................................................................

**FAVOURITE PLAYER:** .......................................................................................................

**Why:** ..............................................................................................................................

..........................................................................................................................................

**BEST GAME YOU'VE SEEN:** ...............................................................................................

..........................................................................................................................................

**Why:** ..............................................................................................................................

..........................................................................................................................................

**LAST PREMIERSHIP:** ........................................................................................................

**THE CLUB YOU LOVE TO HATE:** .........................................................................................

**Why:** ..............................................................................................................................

**(OPPOSITE) FOLLOW THE LEADER:** At the start of every AFL season, the captains and team leaders get together to mark the start of the footy year. **BACK ROW (L-R):** Tom Jonas, Nat Fyfe, Phil Davis, Joe Daniher, Jarrod Witts, Max Gawn, Patrick Cripps, Ben Stratton, Jack Ziebell. **FRONT ROW (L-R):** Joel Selwood, Jarryn Geary, Luke Parker, Trent Cotchin, Shannon Hurn, Scott Pendlebury, Rory Sloane, Dayne Zorko, Jason Johannisen.

| | START OF SEASON | END OF SEASON |
|---|---|---|
| **HEIGHT** | | |
| **WEIGHT** | | |
| **LONGEST KICK (RIGHT FOOT)** | | |
| **LONGEST KICK (LEFT FOOT)** | | |
| **LONGEST HANDBALL** | | |
| **BEST TIME FOR** | 100M | 100M |
| | 50M | 50M |
| | 10M | 10M |

## ALL ABOUT... FOOTY!

**I WAS BORN** in 1858. Various ball games were played across Victoria in that year, but the first recorded match was held in the Richmond Paddock—now the home of the MCG—over two weekends in August, 1858. The teams came from Scotch College and Melbourne Grammar.

**THE FIRST LAWS OF THE GAME** were written in May, 1859. There were just 10 Laws. Ever since, the Laws have constantly evolved. In 2019, variations to the Laws were put into place.

**FIRST TO SCORE TWO GOALS:** In the beginning, the first team to score two goal was declared the winner.

**THE FIRST LAW-MAKERS** were William Hammersley, James Thompson, Tom Wills and Thomas Smith, all members of the Melbourne Football Club. Also present were committee members Alex Bruce, Tom Butterworth, J Sewell and Jerry Bryant.

**WHERE IT ALL HAPPENED:** The law-makers met in a backroom of Jerry Bryant's Parade Hotel, 178 Wellington Parade, East Melbourne, opposite Richmond Park. The hotel, which was later named the MCG hotel, has since been demolished, although the front wall has been retained.

**THE FIRST COMPETITION:** In 1877, the clubs decided that a formal competition should begin under the direction of the Victorian Football Association (VFA). The original clubs in the VFA were Carlton, Melbourne, Hotham, Albert Park, St Kilda, Geelong, Ballarat, Barwon, Beechworth, Castlemaine, Inglewood and Rochester.

**THE VFL BEGINS:** In 1896, eight clubs in the VFA broke away and formed a new competition, the Victorian Football League (VFL), starting in 1897. The clubs were Collingwood, Carlton, Geelong, South Melbourne, Essendon, Fitzroy, St Kilda and Melbourne.

ALL ABOUT... FOOTY!

**THE FIRST PREMIER:** There was no Grand Final in 1897. The top four at the end of the season played each other in a round-robin series. Essendon was the only undefeated team, and was declared the premier team. The first Grand Final was held at St Kilda's Junction Oval in September 1898, and was won by Fitzroy.

**THE MCG (pictured):** The Grand Final was played at the Junction Oval (St Kilda), Lakeside Oval (South Melbourne), and the East Melbourne Ground (now Jolimont rail yards), until 1901. The first decider at the MCG was held in 1902, when Collingwood beat Essendon, the Magpies' first League Flag. Other than for a time during the second World War (1942-45) and in 1991, when Waverley Park played host due to the construction of the MCG's Southern Stand, the Grand Final has been played at the MCG.

**THE BROWNLOW MEDAL (right):** There was no best and fairest player award presented by the VFL until 1924, when the League commemorated one of its finest administrators, Charles Brownlow, and created the Brownlow Medal for 'the fairest and best player' in the competition. The first medal, based on votes of the field umpires, was won by Geelong's Edward 'Carji' Greeves.

**DID YOU KNOW?**
The longest gap between premierships is 72 years, a drought for South Melbourne/Sydney from 1933 to 2005. When coach **Paul Roos (left, with captain Barry Hall)** accepted the Cup on the dais, he shouted to fans: 'Here it is!'

## ALL ABOUT... FOOTY!

**ADDING/LOSING TEAMS:** In 1908, the League expanded, adding Richmond and University clubs. University left the League in 1914, after a winless season. In 1925, Hawthorn, North Melbourne and Footscray (Western Bulldogs) joined. In 1987 the Brisbane Bears and West Coast Eagles joined the VFL, followed by Adelaide (1991), Fremantle (1995), Port Adelaide (1997), Gold Coast (2011) and GWS GIANTS (2012). In 1996, Fitzroy and Brisbane merged to form the Brisbane Lions.

**MORE MEDALS:** In 1979, the League instituted the Norm Smith Medal, to be presented to the best player on Grand Final day, based on votes of selected media. The first winner was Carlton's Wayne Harmes, a grand-nephew of Norm Smith, the Melbourne Coaching Legend. Since 2001, the winning coach has received the Jock McHale Medal.

**THE MEDALS:** L-R: Brownlow Medal, Norm Smith, Rising Star, Jock McHale Medal, Premiership Medal, Coleman Medal.

**THE DRAFT:** Since 1986, players wishing to play League footy have nominated for the National Draft. Clubs then choose the players they believe will suit their needs. The team finishing bottom of the ladder in the previous season has the first pick.

**NATIONAL COMPETITION:** Although Brisbane and West Coast joined the League in 1987, and the Sydney Swans had been playing in NSW since 1982, the Australian Football League, the formal naming of a national competition, wasn't completed until 1990. The first premier in the national competition was Collingwood.

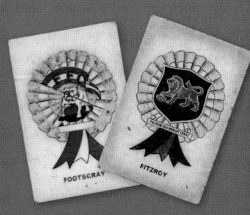

**CHANGES:** The club logos have changed many times through the years, as have club names: Footscray is now the Western Bulldogs, and Fitzroy merged with the Brisbane Bears to become the Brisbane Lions.

**DROUGHT-BREAKER:** Tony Shaw (below) lifts the 1990 Premiership Cup, ending 32 years of Collingwood misery.

## ALL ABOUT... FOOTY!

**WOMEN TOO:** Women have been playing footy for most of the game's life, but it wasn't until 2017 that a national League was created, with eight teams attached to AFL clubs—Carlton, Collingwood, Adelaide, GWS GIANTS, Western Bulldogs, Fremantle, Brisbane Lions and Melbourne. They were joined in 2019 by Geelong and North Melbourne, and joining in 2020 are Gold Coast, Richmond, St Kilda and West Coast.

**PREMIER PREMIERS:** Essendon and Carlton have won the most premierships in the AFL, with 16 wins each; next is Collingwood (15). Since the national competition began, Hawthorn leads the way with five flags, then West Coast (4), and Geelong and Brisbane Lions (3).

**AND ALSO:** Footy is strong in all states, with powerful state Leagues developing quickly after the game began in Victoria (whose state League was formerly the VFA, and is now the VFL). The first was in South Australia (the SANFL began in 1877), then Tasmania (TFL, 1879), NSW (Sydney AFL, formerly NSW Football Association, began in 1880), and Western Australia (WAFL, 1885). Footy was also prominent in Queensland (the QAFL started in 1904) and New Zealand in the 19th Century, but soon was overwhelmed by Rugby and Rugby League.

### IN SHORT

**AFL:** Formed in 1990

**TEAMS:** 18, since 2012

**STATES:** Games are now played in all states and Territories

**OVERSEAS:** In 2013, St Kilda played Sydney in Wellington, NZ; in 2017, Port Adelaide and Gold Coast SUNS played the first game in Shanghai, China

**ROUNDS:** 22

**FINALS:** 9 matches, between eight finalists (since 1994)

**GRAND FINAL:** One, to be played at the MCG until 2057

## THE FINAL EIGHT... HOW IT WORKS

The final eight was introduced in 1994. The current system, providing a double chance to the top four, has been in place since 2000.

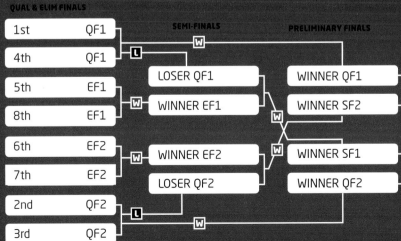

## ALL ABOUT... AFLW

I n February 2017, the inaugural season of the **AFL WOMEN'S (AFLW)** competition began in earnest with eight teams battling it out for the premiership. The women's League has gone from strength to strength since. The foundation clubs were the Adelaide Crows, Brisbane Lions, Carlton, Collingwood, Fremantle Dockers, GWS GIANTS, Melbourne and the Western Bulldogs. In 2019 they were joined by Geelong Cats and North Melbourne, with more clubs, Gold Coast SUNS, Richmond, St Kilda and West Coast Eagles—on the way in 2020. The first official AFLW game was a joyous exhibition of football, attended by 24,568 fans at Carlton's home ground Princes Park—a 'lockout' when enthusiastic supporters filled every available seat. At the end of that first season, Adelaide was crowned the first AFLW premier, beating Brisbane by 6 points in the Grand Final. Crows star Erin Phillips—also a brilliant basketballer who played in WNBA championships and for her country—added to the joy by winning the League's first best and fairest award. Now any young girl who loves footy can get involved in AusKick sessions and sign up for the burgeoning number of junior women's teams at football clubs around Australia. For far too long, people thought footy was just for boys, but it's a sport for everyone!

### QUICK ? QUIZ

In 2017, one of Carlton's AFLW stars kicked four goals in round 1—a better tally than all her Collingwood opponents combined.

**WHAT'S HER NAME?**

**CLUE:** She was the leading goalkicker in the AFLW in 2017 and also took the League's mark of the year.

**WINNING TIME:** Adelaide Crows, AFLW Premiers, 2019

**BACK ROW:** Rheanne Lugg, Chloe Scheer, Nikki Gore, Danielle Ponter, Sarah Allan, Jessica Foley, Jenna McCormick, Maisie Nankivell, Deni Varnhagen, Rhiannon Metcalfe, Jessica Sedunary, Sally Riley, Justine Mules, Dayna Cox, Jasmyn Hewett, Renee Forth, Sarah Perkins. **MIDDLE ROW:** Katelyn Rosenzweig, Sophie Li, Anne Hatchard, Eloise Jones, Ailish Considine, Courtney Cramey, Stevie-Lee Thompson, Hannah Martin, Angela Foley, Marijana Rajcic. **FRONT ROW:** Chelsea Randall, Ebony Marinoff, Erin Phillips

# GIRL POWER!

One of the great things about the success of the AFLW is that it's shown girls all over Australia that footy is a game for everybody! No matter what your age, or where you're from, you can join in the fun and get involved. Like never before, girls and women have a whole new cast of footy stars to look up to. Whether you're sitting at home or in the stands on game day, your cheering and support is appreciated by all the stars of the AFLW. So pull on your guernsey, paint your face, grab a footy and cheer for your favourite players. Who knows, you might end up 'going viral' like the Geelong fans whose moment of joy with Cats star **Georgie Rankin (right)** in 2019 captured the imagination of footy lovers everywhere.

**PEOPLE POWER:** Young Geelong fans were ecstatic to meet their hero Georgie Rankin, and likewise young Pies supporters with Ashleigh Brazill (below).

## DID YOU KNOW?

AFLW differs slightly from the senior AFL game. There are 16 players on the field in AFLW, with 6 interchange players, (18 and 4 in the AFL) and the footy is a little smaller: 530 millimetres around the middle against 555 millimetres in the AFL.

## ALL ABOUT... THE MCG

**T**HE MCG has been the home of footy since the first games were played in 1858, in the paddocks surrounding the great ground. In the beginning, not many games were played there as it was managed by the Melbourne Cricket Club and the cricketers didn't like their turf being roughed up by footy boots, but it didn't take long: the first official footy match was played there in 1859. There have been 18 grandstands surrounding the oval since the first pavilion was built in 1854, holding just 60 fans. In 1876 a reversible stand was built, allowing the seating to be switched from one side to the other. This was burnt down in 1884.

The modern grandstands started with the Great Southern Stand (1991-92), and the Northern Stand (2003-06). Apart from four seasons in the Second World War (1942-45) and in 1991, every Grand Final since 1902 has been played at the MCG, as well as the 1956 Olympics, and 2006 Commonwealth Games, and, of course, the Boxing Day Test. Until 1965, when Richmond moved from Punt Road, Melbourne was the only club to play home games at the MCG; these days, Melbourne, Richmond, Hawthorn and Collingwood call the MCG home.

**QUICK ? QUIZ**

The AFL competition began in 1990. Until the end of the 2018 season, how many AFL Grand Finals have been played at the MCG? Don't trip up.

**CLUE:** Don't forget 1991 and 2010.

### DID YOU KNOW?

The MCG is 161 metres long and 138 metres wide, and has a capacity of 100,024. Hawthorn holds the record for the highest score at the ground (32.24 [216]) against Essendon in 1992. The longest AFL ground in Australia is Darwin's (175 metres), the shortest is the SCG (155 metres) and the narrowest is Geelong's home, the GMHBA Stadium, at 112 metres.

14

# JUMP TO IT

Work out the missing totals. The different coloured footy jumpers have different prices, but with a bit of detective work, and using the row and column totals supplied, you can work out the cost of each jumper. Hint: to make the job a little easier, the cost of the blue jumper is $30.

DEGREE OF DIFFICULTY ★ ★ ★

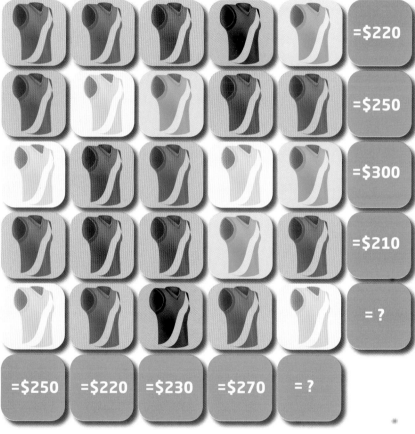

Row totals: =$220, =$250, =$300, =$210, = ?

Column totals: =$250, =$220, =$230, =$270, = ?

## QUICK ? QUIZ

Subiaco Oval was a bog when Freo and Hawthorn took to the ground, and by half-time, a number of clean jumpers were required. Freo had used all players on the bench and one-half needed fresh jumpers; the Hawks had used two of the four interchange players and one-quarter required fresh jumpers.

**HOW MANY PLAYERS WERE ISSUED WITH CLEAN JUMPERS AT HALF TIME?**

**PRIDE:** Melbourne's Max Gawn (below) loves to pull on Melbourne's No.11 guernsey, once worn by club legend, and Gawn's role model and mentor, Jim Stynes.

## DID YOU KNOW?

Since official AFL/VFL matches started in 1897, until round 5 of the 2019 season, 12,719 footballers had played at least one AFL/VFL match. Of that total, 579 had played 200 games or more. That represents just 4.5 per cent of footballers. Tough game!

Australian football was the first footy code in the world to have a set of Laws that all clubs agreed to and played by. Those Laws, written on May 19, 1859, were short and sweet: there were only ten. In other codes, like rugby, soccer, and Gaelic football, the clubs would agree to a set of rules before a game; these could change week by week. In our game, the lawmakers would meet regularly, and make variations, often season by season. The first recorded game of what became Australian football was played between two Melbourne schools, Scotch College and Melbourne Grammar, over two weekends in August 1858, but other games with balls had been played before that official match. The first clubs formed were Melbourne and Geelong, both in 1859, and the first organised competition, with fixtures and finals, was held in 1877, when several clubs formed the Victorian Football Association. Clubs still in the AFL which were part of that competition are Carlton, Melbourne, St Kilda and Geelong. In 1878 Essendon joined, and the following year South Melbourne, now the Sydney Swans. The Australian Football League, founded in 1990, was drawn from the clubs that formed the Victorian Football League in 1897: Carlton, Collingwood, Geelong, Melbourne, St Kilda, Fitzroy (now merged with Brisbane), Essendon, and South Melbourne. The **FIRST OFFICIAL GAME** of AFLW was played on 3 February, 2017. A 'lockout' crowd of 24,568 at Princes Park saw Carlton defeat Collingwood by 25 points.

*Rules of the Melbourne Football Club*
*May, 1859*

*Officers of the Club*
*Committee*
*T. W. Wills Esq*
*W. Hammersley Esq — T. Butterworth*
*— Smith*
*Alex Bruce Esq*
*Hon Treasurer*
*J Sewell Esq*
*Hon Secretary*
*J. B. Thompson Esq*

## QUICK QUIZ

When the national competition began in 1987, which two teams joined from outside Victoria?

**CLUE:** the two teams are the furthest apart of any of the AFL teams.

## DID YOU KNOW?

Fitzroy was one of the founding clubs of the VFL, but merged with the Brisbane Bears in 1996 to become the Brisbane Lions. South Melbourne relocated to Sydney in 1982 and became the Sydney Swans. Footscray changed its name to the Western Bulldogs in 1997, and North Melbourne became the Kangaroos in 1999, but changed back to North Melbourne in 2009.

## ALL ABOUT... THE FOOTBALL

There are so many different types of **FOOTBALLS** in our world. It's a great moment when you get your first real, leather, AFL footy, just like those used in AFL games. The smell of the leather is so wonderful. The footy is so shiny. It's almost a sin to kick it and break that spell.

AFL rules define a footy as being of a symmetrical oval shape with circumferences of between 720 and 730 millimetres (measured around the ends) and 545 and 555 millimetres (around the middle), and to be inflated to a pressure of between 62 and 76 kilopascals . The ball used for AFLW games is slightly smaller, with circumferences of 690 millimetres (measured around the ends) and 530 millimetres (measured around the middle).

An AFL game footy is handmade, using four pieces of Australian cowhide leather surrounding a rubber bladder, and weighs between 450 and 500 grams, fully inflated. The Sherrin brand footy has been made since 1880 and the company now produces more than 100,000 footballs annually. During an AFL season, the AFL will provide no fewer than 832 footballs for its 15 pre-season matches, 8 official practice matches, 176 premiership season matches and 9 finals.

### QUICK ⑦ QUIZ

How many footballs does the AFL provide for each official AFL match?

**CLUE:** How many quarters are there in a match?

545-555mm circumference

720-730mm circumference

LAWS OF FOOTY — Encourage your teammates

### DID YOU KNOW?

You might wonder why some matches use yellow balls, and some red. The answer is simple: yellow is for matches played at night, or twilight, and red is for matches played in the day time. Only the colour of the leather is different—the rest is identical.

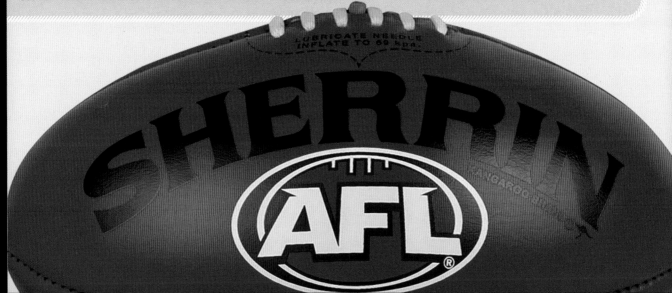

# TRI THIS!

Start with the letter G at the top of the triangle and read down to the next adjoining letter. You'll discover you can spell out the word GOALS a number of times.

**How many can you count?**

DEGREE OF DIFFICULTY  ★ ★ ★

Champion goalkicker John Coleman kicked 537 goals in his 98 games for Essendon, including 12 on debut in round 1, 1949. His average was just under 5.5 goals per game.

**HOW MANY MORE GOALS DID HE NEED TO KICK TO HAVE AN AVERAGE OF 6 GOALS PER GAME?**

G

O O

A A A

L L L L

S S S S S

**CHAMPION GOALKICKER:** John Coleman.

LAWS OF FOOTY

Be determined

## DID YOU KNOW?

The only incidence of a scoreless final quarter in AFL/VFL footy was way back in round 13, 1901, when Fitzroy trailed Collingwood 2.7 (19) to 3.6 (24) going into the last quarter. Neither team added another score.

**ESTABLISHED** 1990

**2019 CAPTAINS** Rory Sloane & Taylor Walker

**SENIOR COACH** Matthew Nicks

O nce the AFL competition was expanded to take in sides from Sydney, Brisbane and Perth, there was never any doubt that a team would be formed in South Australia. Why? Because SA people are crazy about their footy and the game has been part of their sporting culture for a long time. The first side to come out of Adelaide was the Crows, which joined the AFL in 1991. The Crows burst onto the scene and won back-to-back premierships in 1997 and 1998, coached by Malcolm Blight, showing everyone why they belonged. Now the Crows are a powerhouse of the competition, playing in front of packed crowds at the Adelaide Oval every time they play. The Adelaide Crows also joined the AFLW in the inaugural season of the women's League in 2017. The Crows instantly showed everyone they meant business by taking out the 2017 Premiership, and repeated that feat in 2019.

## FROM THE BEGINNING

JOINED THE AFL: 1991

PREMIERSHIPS:
2 - 1997, 1998

AFLW PREMIERSHIPS:
2 - 2017, 2019

GAMES RECORD-HOLDER:
Andrew McLeod (340)

GOALS RECORD-HOLDER:
Tony Modra (440)

JOINED THE AFLW: 2017

## CLUB SONG

(TO THE TUNE OF THE US MARINES HYMN)

We're the pride of
South Australia
And we're known
as the Adelaide Crows
We're courageous
stronger, faster
And respected by our foes
Admiration of the nation
Our determination shows
We're the pride of
South Australia
We're the mighty
Adelaide Crows

### CLAUDE'S MAGIC MOMENTS

**1** Mark Ricciuto became the club's first Brownlow Medalist in 2003 when he shared the award with Sydney's Adam Goodes and Collingwood's Nathan Buckley. It was a three-way tie across the three states!

**2** Darren Jarman's performances in Grand Finals for the Crows are masterpieces in the art of forward play. In the 1997 decider he booted five goals in the last quarter—six for the game—as the Crows sealed their maiden Premiership against St Kilda. Jarman was dominant again in 1998, booting five.

**3** Andrew McLeod was a champion of Adelaide's greatest era, a point best illustrated by his back-to-back Norm Smith Medal wins in the Crows' 1997 and 1998 AFL premierships. With 340 appearances for the Crows, McLeod is also Adelaide's games record-holder. That record will take some beating!

Claude the Crow >

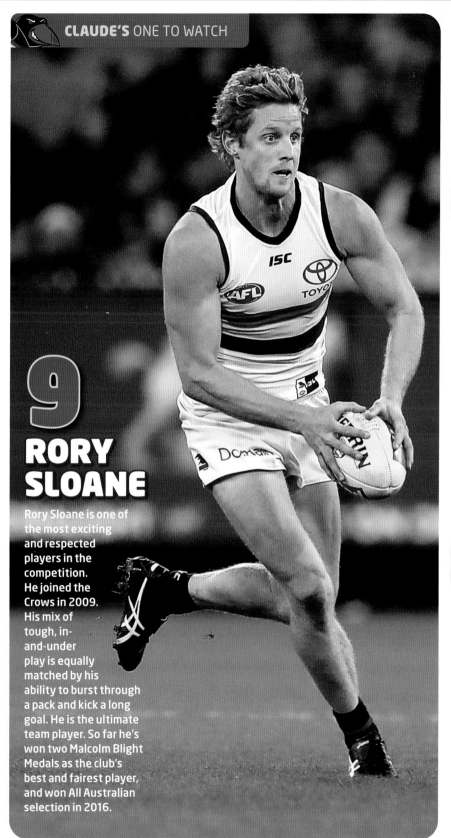

**CLAUDE'S** ONE TO WATCH

# 9
# RORY SLOANE

Rory Sloane is one of the most exciting and respected players in the competition. He joined the Crows in 2009. His mix of tough, in-and-under play is equally matched by his ability to burst through a pack and kick a long goal. He is the ultimate team player. So far he's won two Malcolm Blight Medals as the club's best and fairest player, and won All Australian selection in 2016.

# QUICK QUIZ

The Crows' bustling midfielder/ forward Tom Lynch, led Adelaide's goal kicking in 2013. In that season he also kicked his personal best goal tally in a game.

**HOW MANY GOALS DID HE KICK AND WHO WAS IT AGAINST?**

**CLUE:** The team was new to the competition and it was in double figures!

**ANSWER**

# DID YOU KNOW?

Malcolm Blight had coached Geelong to three losing Grand Finals before taking the reins at Adelaide in 1997. His impact was rapid. The Crows had finished 12th in 1996, but under Blight's quirky coaching, they would win back-to-back flags in 1997-98. Blight, one of the game's greatest players—at Woodville and North Melbourne— winning a Magarey Medal (1972) and a Brownlow Medal (1978), was elevated to Legend in the Australian Football Hall of Fame in 2017.

# AFC.COM.AU

**CLAUDE'S** ONE TO WATCH

# 13

# ERIN PHILLIPS

Erin Phillips is an Australian sporting superstar, having arrived in footy following a stellar career in basketball, where she won two WNBA championships, and for her country, a World Championship gold medal and an Olympic silver medal.

Phillips has followed in the footsteps of her father, Greg, an All Australian footballer who played at centre half-back for Port Adelaide (343 games) and Collingwood (84 games). With the establishment of the AFLW in 2017, Erin Phillips has taken the competition by storm, winning every AFLW award, including two competition B&F's, and two best on ground performances in Adelaide's winning Grand Finals—2017 and 2019. That 2019 win came after she had been injured in the third quarter and could take no further part in the game! Happily, she looks set to play for the Crows again in 2020.

**2019 CAPTAINS** Chelsea Randall & Erin Phillips

**2020 SENIOR COACH** Matthew Clarke

The Crows have been one of the success stories of the AFLW, winning both the inaugural premiership in 2017, and also the 2019 competition. So dominant were the likes of Chelsea Randall, Jess Foley, Stevie-Lee Thompson, Marijana Rajcic and Ebony Marinoff, almost a quarter of the 2019 All-Australian squad of 40 players was made up of Crows!

# WHAT PLAYERS EAT

## QUICK ? QUIZ

Pick the odd one out: apples, pears, bananas, rhubarb, oranges, mangos?

**CLUE:** It's the one with a stalk.

**A**FL players are disciplined with their diets, and all clubs have trained dietitians on staff to advise players of all shapes and sizes what food will best provide them with the right amount of energy, and muscle mass—whether it's pre-season, in-season training, or game day. As with all sport, you need to eat the right foods, and take the right amount of liquid, to ensure you have truckloads of energy so you can run hard, tackle powerfully, withstand hard hits, and, ultimately, perform at your best for the four quarters.

Diet is based on science—exchanging food for energy stored in your muscles—and the best energy source comes from carbohydrates, like breads, cereals, pasta, fruit and vegetables. On game day, finish your meal three or four hours before game time to ensure your stomach is empty, but your energy is high. Players will also avoid fats, and add to their protein intake with lean meats, fish, skinless chicken, smoothies and cheese. Sadly, that means keeping clear of chocolate, chips and most takeaway foods. When you are looking for something sweet, go for your favourite fruit or vegetable to provide the hit you need. It might sound tough, but there's no better feeling than having your body tuned like a racing car.

Preserving energy has also been assisted by the use of the interchange, bringing players off at regular intervals to allow them to run out every quarter.

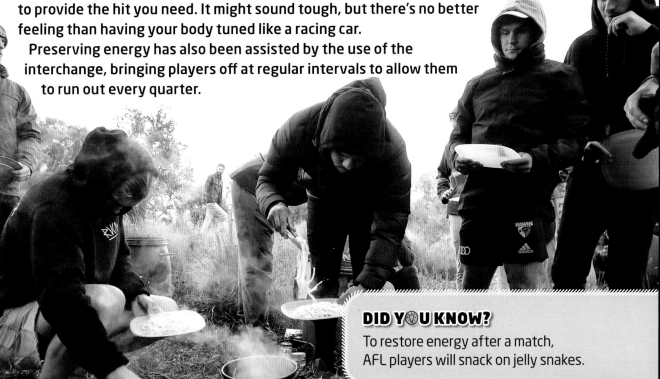

## DID Y☺U KNOW?

To restore energy after a match, AFL players will snack on jelly snakes.

REAL

FAKE!

**DOUBLE UP:** Chelsea Randall (left) and Erin Phillips celebrate the 2019 premiership with their coach, Matthew Clarke.

**PICKING SOMETHING AS OBVIOUS AS COLOURS IS ONE THING, BUT CAN YOU SPOT THE TEN DIFFERENCES BETWEEN THESE PHOTOGRAPHS?**

AFL WOMENS
COMPETITION
2019
PREMIERSHIP CUP
WON BY

**ESTABLISHED** Fitzroy 1883, Brisbane Bears 1986, Brisbane Lions 1996

**CAPTAIN** Dayne Zorko

**SENIOR COACH** Chris Fagan

The Brisbane Lions haven't always been 'roaring' around the Gabba, and they haven't always been the Lions. Brisbane was once known as the Brisbane Bears and, until 1992, played at Carrara on the Gold Coast. At the end of 1996, the Fitzroy Lions, which joined the AFL/VFL way back in 1897, merged with the Bears and the Bears became the Lions. Got that? But did you know that Fitzroy used to be known as the Maroons (after the club colour) and the Gorillas? The Lions roared into the early 2000s winning three flags in three years from 2001 to 2003—only three other clubs had done that before then (Carlton, Collingwood [which won four straight from 1927], Melbourne [twice]) with the Hawks joining that group with their wins in 2013-15! Now the Lions have one of the most exciting young teams in the League with a swag of superstars bursting through. In 2017, the Lions also joined the AFLW competition and finished in 2017 and 2018 strongly, both times losing the Grand Final by only 6 points.

## ROY'S MAGIC MOMENTS

**1** Grand Final day in 2001, 2002 and 2003—obviously! Glory came with wins over Essendon (26 points), Collingwood (9 points) and the Pies again (50 points).

**2** In 2001 and 2002, the Lions produced Brownlow Medallists: Jason Akermanis and Simon Black both took out the award, joining their captain Michael Voss who had also won it in 1996, in a tie with Essendon's James Hird.

**3** In round 13, 2013, at the Gabba, the Lions completed the equal 9th biggest comeback in League history. At the 22-minute mark of the third quarter they trailed Geelong by 52 points. The Lions surged home kicking 10 of the last 11 goals, to win by 5 points.

Roy >

## FROM THE BEGINNING

FITZROY FORMED: 1883
FITZROY JOINED VFL/AFL: 1897
BRISBANE BEARS FORMED: 1986
BRISBANE BEARS JOINED VFL/AFL: 1987
BEARS AND FITZROY MERGED: 1996
VFL PREMIERSHIPS (FITZROY): 8 - 1898, 1899, 1904, 1905, 1913, 1916, 1922, 1944.
AFL PREMIERSHIPS (BRISBANE LIONS): 3 - 2001, 2002, 2003
GAMES RECORD-HOLDER: Simon Black (322)
GOALS RECORD-HOLDER: Jonathan Brown (594)
JOINED THE AFLW: 2017

## CLUB SONG

(TO THE TUNE OF THE FRENCH NATIONAL ANTHEM, LA MARSEILLAISE)

We are the pride of Brisbane town
We wear maroon, blue and gold
We will always fight for victory
Like Fitzroy and the Bears of old
All for one and one for all
We will answer to the call
Go Lions, Brisbane Lions
We'll kick the winning score
You'll hear our mighty roar

### ROY'S ONE TO WATCH

# 15
# DAYNE ZORKO

Dayne Zorko is the definition of a pocket rocket. While only standing at 175cm, the man from Surfers Paradise can take over any game with his extreme speed and his remarkable goal sense. In 2018, he took out his fourth consecutive club champion trophy, adding to his 2017 All Australian guernsey.

# QUICK QUIZ

Senior coach Chris Fagan came to Brisbane after an assistant coaching role at Melbourne (1999-2007), and then a period of football management at Hawthorn (2008-16).

**WHERE WAS HIS FIRST COACHING JOB?**

**CLUE:** It's not on the mainland.

....................................................

**ANSWER**

....................................................

# DID YOU KNOW?

The Lions have had nine Brownlow Medallists yet their players have won 11 medals between them. How can that be? Enter **Haydn Bunton (right)**. Ever heard of him? Bunton was a champion player for Fitzroy from 1931 to 1937, when he won three Brownlows— two in his first two years. Not too bad!

# LIONS.COM.AU

ROY'S ONE TO WATCH

# 13
# KATE LUTKINS

It's little wonder that Kate Lutkins won the 'most courageous player' award in the Lions' inaugural season of 2017—when the All Australian defender steps away from the football field, she's a Private in the Australian Army. Quietly-spoken Lutkins proves that match-winners aren't always the flashy players. 'You've got to have your teammates' back no matter what and work hard for each other,' she once said. And that is Lutkins: the ideal teammate.

**2019 CAPTAIN**
Leah Kaslar

**2020 COACH**
Craig Starcevich

The Lions were one of the eight foundation teams granted ALFW licences for the 2017 season, with former Collingwood and Brisbane star Craig Starcevich as their inaugural coach. They were Grand Finalists in the first two seasons of AFLW, and will be looking to go one better than that in 2020.

# LUCKY LOCKER

The Premiership Cup is in one of these footy lockers and you need to get it onto centre stage at the MCG for the presentation ceremony. You don't have time to hunt through all four lockers; you need it now! The lockers are part of the locker room of the players who have won the Norm Smith Medal.

The Cup is in the locker of the Brownlow Medallist who also won the Norm Smith Medal.

## QUICK ? QUIZ

The Premiership Cup was first presented in which year?

**CLUE:** It was three years after the Melbourne Olympics, and presented to Melbourne, which had just registered its 10th Grand Final win.

1 2 3 4

Wayne Harmes • Gary Ayres • Shaun Hart • Simon Black

**DEGREE OF DIFFICULTY** ★☆☆

## DID Y♥U KNOW?

The Premiership Cup is silver-plated on the outside and gold-plated on the inside. It weighs 8.5 kilograms, including the wooden base, and is 55 centimetres tall. Vin Formosa, of Cash's in Melbourne, has made the Cup since 1986 and each cup takes him 85 hours to craft. The Cup is still made according to the original design supplied by Sir Kenneth Luke, who was VFL president from 1956 to 1971.

 Get to the contest

BELIEVE IT OR NOT

# SHE'LL BE APPLES

## QUICK ? QUIZ
Who kicked the point after the siren in a 1996 preliminary final to put the Swans into their first Grand Final in 51 years?

An apple potentially changed the result of a match and a club's hunt for a finals berth in 1970. It was at Kardinia Park (as GMHBA Stadium was called then), in round 20 of the 22-round home and away season, 10 minutes from the final siren. Famously accurate Cat Doug Wade—he kicked 1,057 goals in his 267 games—lined up for goal from 35 metres out on a slight angle. He looked certain to put the Cats in front, until... an apple had the Cats crying over spilt milk. With the ball in flight and on target, a fan threw an apple core that hit the footy, causing it to change direction and go through for a point. The Swans won a tight one, 11.15 (81) to 10.14 (74) and went on to squeeze into the final four. The Cats finished fifth.

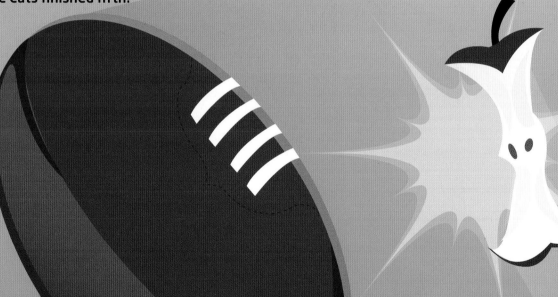

## DID YOU KNOW?
The Bombers hold the record when it comes to finals thrashings. They beat the Pies by a massive 133 points in their 1984 preliminary final clash. Not surprisingly, they went on to win the flag.

# AGE FACTOR

Tell a friend you're going to guess their age and the number of times they hope their team will win this season, then follow the instructions below. This is guaranteed to impress! The number you end up with will comprise the wins followed by their age.

DEGREE OF DIFFICULTY ★ ☆ ☆

The oldest Brownlow Medallist, Barry Round (right), attempts to outmark Bernie Quinlan.

Put your body on the line for the team

## QUICK ? QUIZ

Two teenagers played in the 2018 Grand Final—one from West Coast and one from the Pies.

**WHO WAS THE YOUNGER?**

**CLUE:** He also took out the NAB AFL Rising Star Award in his debut season at AFL level.

## ⓘNSTRUCTIONS

1. Ask a friend to think of the number of times they would like their team to win this season.

2. Tell them to multiply that number by 2, add 5 and then multiply by 50.

3. Ask them to add to that total the 4-digit number of the current year.

4. If they have already had their birthday this year, tell them to subtract 250; if they haven't had their birthday, they should subtract 251.

5. Ask them to subtract the 4-digit number of the year they were born.

**ESTABLISHED** 1864

**CAPTAINS** Patrick Cripps & Sam Docherty

**SENIOR COACH** David Teague

The Carlton Football Club is almost as old as the game itself. It was formed in 1864, just a few years after the first recorded game of Australian Football was played between Melbourne Grammar School and Scotch College in August 1858. In an early competition known as the Challenge Cup, Carlton wore orange caps, then added a blue band, which is how the navy blue was born. Carlton was an original member of the Victorian Football Association in 1877, and one of eight clubs to break away and form the VFL for the start of the 1897 season. Carlton has had huge success, winng a League record 16 flags, equal with Essendon. Carlton is the first team to win three straight flags (1906-08), was the first club to appoint a coach (John Worrall in 1902) and has been the home to many legends of the game such as John Nicholls, Alex Jesaulenko, Bruce Doull, Craig Bradley, Stephen Kernahan, Stephen Silvagni and Chris Judd. Carlton was one of the eight clubs chosen in the first season of AFLW and already boasts superstars like Tayla Harris and Darcy Vescio.

### NINA'S MAGIC MOMENTS

**1** One of the great matches in League history was the 1970 Grand Final, when Carlton came from 44 points down at half-time to overrun Collingwood in the second half. The Blues kicked 13.4 after half-time to Collingwood's 4.4 to win by 10 points.

**2** The mark by Carlton's Alex Jesaulenko over Collingwood's Graham 'Jerker' Jenkin in the 1970 Grand Final would have made Superman green with envy. Mike Williamson's call of: 'JESAULENKO! YOU BEAUTY!' will never be forgotten.

**3** Carlton's greatest era might have been between 1979 and 1982, when the Blues won three flags, directed by three different coaches: Alex Jesaulenko, captain-coach in 1979, Peter Jones (1980, finished fourth), and David Parkin for the 1981-82 back-to-back Premierships.

# FROM THE BEGINNING

**CLUB FORMED:** 1864
**JOINED THE VFL/AFL:** 1897
**PREMIERSHIPS: 16** – 1906-08, 1914-15, 1938, 1945, 1947, 1968, 1970, 1972, 1979, 1981-82, 1987, 1995
**GAMES RECORD-HOLDER:** Craig Bradley (375)
**GOALS RECORD-HOLDER:** Stephen Kernahan (738)
**JOINED THE AFLW:** 2017

# CLUB SONG

**(TO THE TUNE OF LILY OF LAGUNA)**

We are the Navy Blues
We are the old dark Navy Blues
We're the team that never lets you down
We're the only team old Carlton knows
With all the champions they like to send us
We'll keep our end up
And they will know that they've been playing
Against the famous old dark Blues

Captain Carlton >

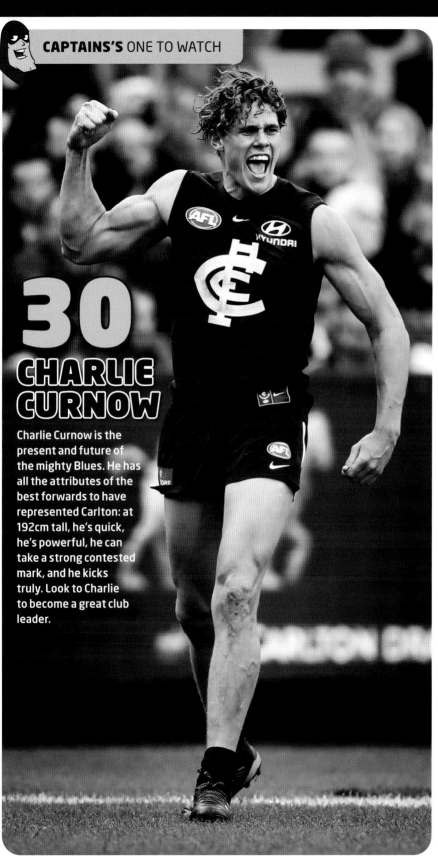

**CAPTAINS'S** ONE TO WATCH

# 30
# CHARLIE CURNOW

Charlie Curnow is the present and future of the mighty Blues. He has all the attributes of the best forwards to have represented Carlton: at 192cm tall, he's quick, he's powerful, he can take a strong contested mark, and he kicks truly. Look to Charlie to become a great club leader.

Navy Nina ›

# QUICK QUIZ

In 2017 the Curnows were the only brothers on the Carlton list. In 2018 another set of brothers, with great links to the Carlton story, joined them.

## WHO ARE THEY?

**CLUE:** Their grandfather and father both played in Carlton premierships (1968, 1970, 1987, 1995).

**ANSWER**

# DID YOU KNOW?

Carlton's training ground is at Princes Park, right in the heart of Carlton. The Blues played their home games there from 1897 to 2005 until they moved to Marvel Stadium at Docklands. They now play at the mighty MCG and at Marvel Stadium.

# CARLTONFC. COM.AU

CARLTON

CLUB ZONE

NINA'S ONE TO WATCH

**2019 CAPTAIN**
Brianna Davey

**2020 SENIOR COACH**
Daniel Harford

# 10
# SARAH HOSKING

Carlton midfielder Sarah Hosking is one of the AFLW's leading ball-winners and tacklers. In round 2 of the 2018 season, the fearless Hosking laid 16 ferocious tackles to keep her GIANTS opponents on their toes. They could have been forgiven for thinking they were seeing double: Hosking's identical twin sister, Jess, is also a star for Carlton. Both play with the Hosking trademark courage, going hard for the ball and, so often, ending up with it!

One of the glamour clubs of the competition thanks to the history and tradition of the Carlton Football Club, the Blues were foundation members of the AFLW. With the likes of Darcy Vescio and the Hosking twins leading the way, and former Hawthorn and Carlton midfielder Daniel Harford at the helm, they have become a power, making the Grand Final in their third season.

Navy Nina >

# DEFENCE FORCE

The forward 50 is pretty congested with the Goannas (the brown team) opting to play a loose man in defence. But there is a way to separate all the players. By drawing four straight lines across the field (to help you, we've supplied one line and red dots to indicate where the other three lines start and end), you can separate each of the players.

**DEGREE OF DIFFICULTY** ★ ★ ★

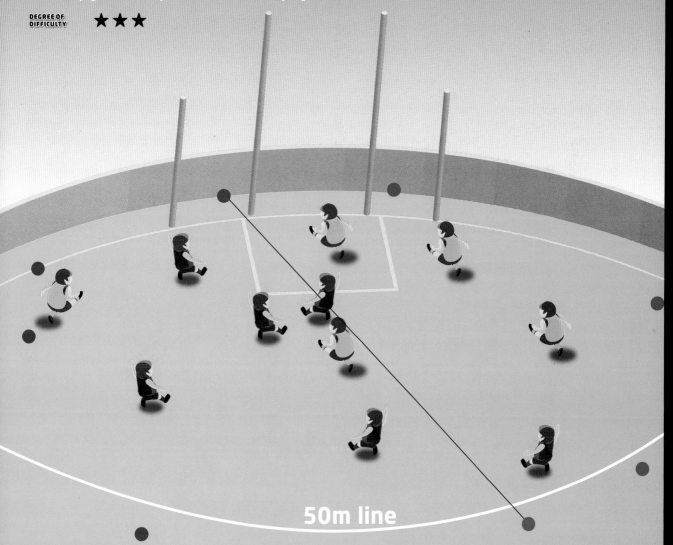

50m line

## DID Y☺U KNOW?
The 50-metre arcs that you see on all the footy grounds today were first introduced in 1986 so that fans and media commentators could more accurately gauge the length of kicks for goal.

# CAPTAIN/VICE-CAPTAIN/COACH

Every club has a **COACH**, a **CAPTAIN**, and at least one **VICE-CAPTAIN**. Captain comes from a Latin word, 'caput', meaning 'head'. The captain is the team's head. Often the captain is called the skipper, which is a word borrowed from shipping. The old English word for 'ship' was 'scip', and the man in charge, the captain, was the 'scipper'. Vice, as in vice-captain, is also a Latin word—the same word that appears in the well-known phrase, vice versa. Vice literally means 'by change' and has come to mean 'the next in line'. Believe it or not, the word coach is derived from the name of a Hungarian village called Kocs, where a new-style carriage was developed way back in the 15th Century. The carriage was called, in a shortened term, a 'kocsi'. This word spread throughout Europe and was used to refer to all carriages. In English, kocsi became 'coche' and then coach. So how did coach become a footy coach? Slang got the ballgame rolling. The link is that a coach would 'carry' his student through exams and a player through a sporting context. Clever, huh?

## QUICK ? QUIZ

Who holds the AFL record for most games as captain?

**CLUE:** His nickname is 'Sticks' and he played for the Blues.

## DID Y●U KNOW?

Captains and coaches were often one and the same person. The last captain-coach was Malcolm Blight, who coached and captained North Melbourne until round 16, 1981, when he handed over to Barry Cable. In the same season, Alex Jesaulenko was captain-coach at St Kilda until round 8; he then coached from the bench. Jesaulenko is the last captain-coach to lead a Premiership team— Carlton in 1979.

**LEADERSHIP:** Alex Jesaulenko (pictured) and Malcolm Blight were the last of footy's playing coaches.

## ALL ABOUT... FOOTY'S GREATEST PHOTO

This photo of Alex Jesaulenko pulling down his spectacular 'mark of the century' is regarded by many as footy's greatest photo. In fact, more than one photographer took a variation of this shot—examples by Clive McKinnon, Dennis Bull, Alan Funnell, Rennie Ellis and Bruce Howard are the best known. 'Jezza' leaped over Collingwood's Graeme 'Jerker' Jenkin to take the mark, and the game in question—the 1970 Grand Final—turned into one of the greatest of all. The Blues came back from 44 points down to win a thrilling premiership, watched by a record crowd of 121,696 fans.

### QUICK ❓ QUIZ

The final scoreline in the 1970 Grand Final was 17.9 (111) to 14.17 (101). Carlton's Ted Hopkins kicked four second-half goals.

**IF OTHER TEAMMATES CONTRIBUTED 10 GOALS, HOW MANY DID THE OTHER MAIN CONTRIBUTOR, ALEX JESAULENKO, MANAGE TO KICK?**

### DID Y⦿U KNOW?

The record crowd set in the 1970 Grand Final will never be broken, as the maximum attendance possible is now just over 100,000. Why? Changes to the ground reduced the standing room capacity, with most patrons now purchasing reserved seats.

LAWS OF FOOTY — Get teammates involved

**POWER PLAY:** Carlton star Tayla Harris is renowned for her perfect kicking action.

# COLOUR ME IN!

# COLOUR ME IN!

**ESTABLISHED** 1892

**CAPTAIN** Scott Pendlebury

**SENIOR COACH** Nathan Buckley

Collingwood is the AFL club that people either love or hate and it has been that way since the Mapgies entered the League as one of its foundation clubs in 1897. In their early days, the Pies were referred to as the 'Flatties' because the suburb of Collingwood is flat! But it didn't take them long to earn a reputation for sharpness on the field. They won four flags in a row from 1927 to 1930—a record that stands today. After winning their 13th flag in 1958—to stop Melbourne equalling their record of four straight wins—they earned the nickname the 'Colliwobbles' after losing the next eight Grand Finals they played in! They eventually broke the drought in 1990, led by coach Leigh Matthews and captain Tony Shaw. In 2010 the Pies made it 15 flags, winning the Grand Final re-match after a draw with St Kilda. In 2017 the Magpies fielded a team in the initial season of the AFLW.

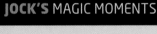

**JOCK'S** MAGIC MOMENTS

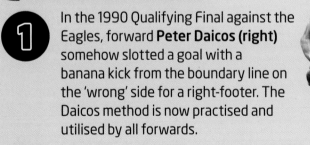

**1** In the 1990 Qualifying Final against the Eagles, forward **Peter Daicos (right)** somehow slotted a goal with a banana kick from the boundary line on the 'wrong' side for a right-footer. The Daicos method is now practised and utilised by all forwards.

**2** Collingwood's blistering first half in the 2018 Preliminary Final against the flag favourite Richmond was a sight to behold, with the Texas-born mature-aged recruit Mason Cox tearing the game apart with his huge marks and goals.

**3** Who could forget Heath Shaw's superb smother as Nick Riewoldt was about to goal from metres out in the first quarter of the 2010 Grand Final rematch? It was a sign of things to come as Collingwood went on to win comfortably.

Jock 'One Eye' McPie >

## FROM THE BEGINNING

**CLUB FORMED:** 1892
**JOINED THE VFL/AFL:** 1897
**PREMIERSHIPS:**
**15** - 1902-03, 1910, 1917, 1919, 1927-30, 1935-36, 1953, 1958, 1990, 2010
**GAMES RECORD-HOLDER:** Tony Shaw (313)
**GOALS RECORD-HOLDER:** Gordon Coventry (1299)
**JOINED THE AFLW:** 2017

## CLUB SONG

(TO THE TUNE OF GOODBYE DOLLY GRAY)

Good Old Collingwood forever
We know how to play the game
Side by side we stick together
To uphold the Magpies' name
Hear the barrackers a shouting
As all barrackers should.
Oh the Premiership's a cakewalk
For the good old Collingwood

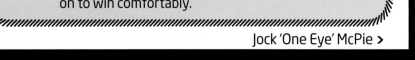

JOCK'S ONE TO WATCH

# 4
# BRODIE GRUNDY

Brodie Grundy has become one of the best ruckman in the game. Earning his second All Australian in 2019, the sky is the limit for the 203cm Grundy. Grundy is the classic modern ruckman, who not only competes in the air and at stoppages, but has supreme skills around the ground.

COLLINGWOOD

# QUICK QUIZ

Collingwood's 2010 premiership win came after its second draw in a Grand Final.

**WHO WAS THE FIRST ONE AGAINST?**

**CLUE:** The other team 'jumped' away with the win.

.............................................

ANSWER

.............................................

# DID YOU KNOW?

The Collingwood big man, **Mason Cox (right)**, has taken an unusual route to the AFL, being recruited from Oklahoma State University in the USA. He is the tallest player measured at an AFL Draft Combine, standing at 211.4cm. He used all of that height in the 2018 Preliminary Final against Richmond, taking eight contested marks and kicking three goals.

# COLLINGWOODFC. COM.AU

CLUB ZONE

**COLLINGWOOD**

CLUB ZONE

# 10
# ASHLEIGH BRAZILL

So many kids grow up dreaming of playing for the Pies, but Ashleigh Brazill has achieved the feat twice over, playing for Collingwood in both netball and footy! That made her the first athlete in Australia to play two codes for the one club. As a netballer, the wing-defence won Collingwood's 2018 best and fairest award and has been picked to play for her country. In the 2019 AFLW season, the speedy defender was nothing less than a star, winning All Australian honours in a stellar season.

**2019 CAPTAIN**
Steph Chiocci

**2020 SENIOR COACH**
Stephen Symonds

Whenever the Magpies take the field, one thing is certain: there will be hordes of fans cheering on the women in black and white. Like the men's team, Collingwood's AFLW squad trains at the impressive Olympic Park facility, and with stars like skipper Steph Chiocci, Emma Grant, Ash Brazill and Jaimee Lambert leading the charge, they're a team of the future.

## ALL ABOUT... JUMPER RECORDS

It's hard to imagine, but players didn't wear numbers in the earliest days of AFL/VFL football. The first time players were identified by **NUMBERS** was in 1903, when Fitzroy played Collingwood. And here's one for trivia fans: it was also the first League match played in Sydney! Numbers weren't made compulsory until 1912, the same year the Football Record was published. The highest number to appear in an AFL game is No.67, worn by a host of players including Lance Franklin, Daniel Wells and Shaun Burgoyne, during Indigenous rounds through the years—those one-off jumpers commemorated the 1967 referendum to include Indigenous Australians in the census. It's not common today to see players wearing numbers in the 50s, although North Melbourne star Ben Brown wears No.50. Few numbers are more famous than No.29, worn a record 432 times by North Melbourne's Brent 'Boomer' Harvey, and 403 times by Richmond's five-time premiership hero Kevin Bartlett. Some famous players made their debuts in unfamiliar numbers: goal-kicking legend Tony Lockett (4), wore No.37 on his St Kilda debut in 1983, while James Hird (5) wore No.49 for the Bombers in 1992 and Leigh Matthews (3) wore No.53 in his first season (1969), No.32 in his second, and didn't wear his famous No.3 until 1972.

Always be well prepared  LAWS OF FOOTY

### DID YOU KNOW?
Gordon Coventry kicked 1,299 goals in 306 games for Collingwood between 1920 and 1937. He also wore nine different numbers—3, 5, 6, 7, 8, 9, 10, 22 and 29.

## QUICK ? QUIZ

For four decades, Geelong and North Melbourne legend Doug Wade held the record for the most goals in No.23, with 834.

**BUT WHICH MODERN STAR HAS PASSED HIM?**

**CLUE:** He plays for the Swans and won two premierships with the Hawks.

**1967:** Daniel Wells of the Magpies wears the number 67 to commemorate the 1967 referendum to include Indigenous Australians in the census.

# JUMPER JUMBLE

They did things differently in the old days. Collingwood's champion full-back of the 1930s and 40s, the late Jack Regan (right), wore 11 different jumper numbers during his 196 matches for the Magpies. He was a great player and is a member of Collingwood's Team of the Century. No other player in the history of the game has had so many numbers on his back. Imagine if he was your favourite player! You'd never be able to keep up!

## DID YOU KNOW?

Captain Jack Regan wore the No.1 jumper in 1941 and 1943. It was part of a Collingwood tradition that began in 1936 when the club offered captain Harry Collier, who had worn No.8 as captain in 1935, the right to the No.1 guernsey. The custom continued until 1979, when captain Ray Shaw decided to retain his No.23 jumper. From 1936 to 1978, only Pat Fricker (1944) and John Henderson (part of 1965) did not eventually take up the option of wearing No.1. The last Magpie captain to take the No.1 was Len Thompson in 1978.

16 — 1936
23 — 1940
1 — 1941, 43
32 — 1932
27 — 1930-31
25 — 1935
24 — 1934
20 — 1933
18 — 1938-39
22 — 1937
2 — 1946

**QUICK ? QUIZ**
Mick Malthouse has the record for the most games as coach, but who holds the record for the most games as a player and coach combined?
**CLUE:** He played for Richmond and coached Essendon and GWS GIANTS.

**GREATEST COACH:** Jock McHale coached Collingwood to eight premierships and played in another.

Coaching can be one of the hardest jobs in football—everyone thinks they know how their team needs to be coached and who should be playing where. **GREAT COACHES** have special characteristics that earn them the players' respect. They need to be teachers, motivators, strategists and spokesmen. One of the greatest coaches of all time, Collingwood's James 'Jock' McHale, coached the Magpies 714 times from 1912 to 1949 and won eight premierships! McHale's 714-game League record was eventually broken by another Pies coach, Michael Malthouse, whose coaching career at the Bulldogs, West Coast, Collingwood and Carlton totalled 718 games and three premierships. He also played 174 League games for St Kilda and Richmond, winning a premiership with the Tigers in 1980.

**LAWS OF FOOTY** Finish off the hard work

**DID YOU KNOW?**
Jock McHale was born in New South Wales and played 261 games for Collingwood. He coached the Magpies in 714 games—a span that included World Wars I and II and the depression in the 1930s. The premiership coach from each season is awarded the Jock McHale Medal in his honour.

**ESTABLISHED** 1872

**CAPTAIN** Dyson Heppell

**SENIOR COACH** John Worsfold

In its early days, the club was known as the Same Olds and it has certainly been the 'same old' story of ongoing glory through the years. The club's nickname changed to the Bombers after the club moved to Windy Hill, which is close to Essendon Airport. Essendon has produced some of the game's greatest players, with triple Brownlow Medallist Dick Reynolds at the top of the pile. Reynolds remains the youngest winner of the Brownlow. His on-ball companion, Bill Hutchison, won two Brownlows. Essendon was also an important club to promote Indigenous players, with trailblazers Michael Long and Gavin Wanganeen (another Brownlow winner). The Bombers share the record of 16 premierships with Carlton, with their most recent flag won in 2000, a season in which they lost just one match out of 25. Now coached by former Eagles Premiership captain and coach, John Worsfold, the Bombers are geared up to return to the top.

### SKEETA'S MAGIC MOMENTS

**1** Essendon registered the greatest comeback in AFL history at the MCG in round 16, 2001, when they came from 69 points down against the Roos at the 10-minute mark of the second term, to run over their opponents and win by 12 points.

**2** **John Coleman (right)** kicked a record 12.2 on debut in round 1, 1949, against Hawthorn, jumpstarting a phenomenal career in which he would kick 537 goals in 98 games before a knee injury ended his career. He averaged 5.5 goals a match!

**3** On ANZAC day, 2009, Essendon was down by 14 points in pouring rain with only five minutes remaining. Goals to Leroy Jetta and Ricky Dyson brought the Bombers to within a point of the Magpies, before David Zaharakis goalled from the 50-metre mark to complete a stunning victory.

Skeeta >

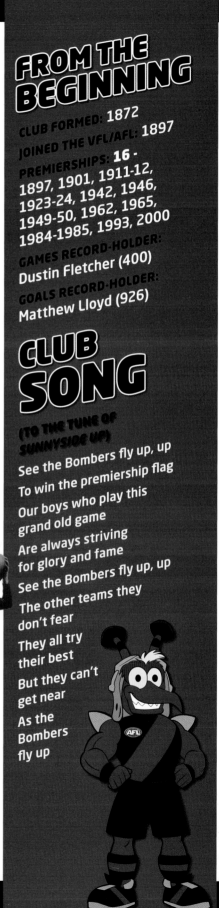

## FROM THE BEGINNING

**CLUB FORMED:** 1872
**JOINED THE VFL/AFL:** 1897
**PREMIERSHIPS: 16 -**
1897, 1901, 1911-12, 1923-24, 1942, 1946, 1949-50, 1962, 1965, 1984-1985, 1993, 2000
**GAMES RECORD-HOLDER:** Dustin Fletcher (400)
**GOALS RECORD-HOLDER:** Matthew Lloyd (926)

## CLUB SONG

**(TO THE TUNE OF SUNNYSIDE UP)**

See the Bombers fly up, up
To win the premiership flag
Our boys who play this grand old game
Are always striving for glory and fame
See the Bombers fly up, up
The other teams they don't fear
They all try their best
But they can't get near
As the Bombers fly up

# 21 DYSON HEPPELL

Captain Dyson Heppell is not only one of the League's premier midfielders but is also one of the toughest players in the game. With his long blond locks, dashing running and kicking style, he is impossible to miss on the field. He is Essendon's only winner of the Rising Star award (2011), was a 2014 All Australian and won Essendon's best and fairest award in 2014.

# QUICK QUIZ

Kevin Sheedy (below), coached Essendon for 29 seasons and 635 games, both club records.

**WHAT OTHER TEAM DID HE COACH?**

**CLUE:** They are new guys on the block.

........................................

**ANSWER**

........................................

# DID YOU KNOW?

Essendon boasts the two biggest finals wins ever. The Bombers beat Collingwood by 133 points in the 1984 preliminary final at Waverley Park and flogged the Kangaroos by 125 points in a qualifying final at the MCG in 2000.

# ESSENDONFC. COM.AU

# BRAINBUSTER

Three children, whose given names are Jack, Sophie and Sam, and whose surnames, not necessarily in the same order, are Notting, Porter and Johnson, buy a scarf, a beanie and a flag. The prices, not necessarily in order, are $8, $9 and $10. From the clues below, can you match the surnames, items and prices to the given names?

**DEGREE OF DIFFICULTY**  ★ ★ ★

## CLUES

1. Sophie is not the person whose surname is Notting.

2. The child named Notting did not spend $8 on an item.

3. The flag was bought by the child whose surname is Porter.

4. The scarf was bought by Jack.

5. The beanie was not bought by Sam.

6. The beanie cost $10.

| GIVEN NAME | SURNAME | ITEM | PRICE |
|---|---|---|---|
| JACK | | | |
| SOPHIE | | | |
| SAM | | | |

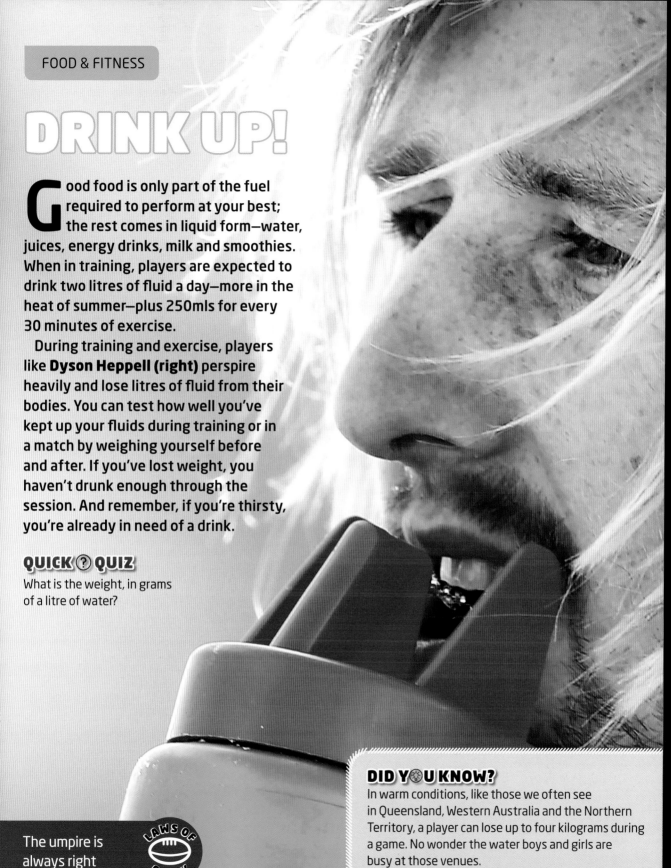

# DRINK UP!

**G**ood food is only part of the fuel required to perform at your best; the rest comes in liquid form—water, juices, energy drinks, milk and smoothies. When in training, players are expected to drink two litres of fluid a day—more in the heat of summer—plus 250mls for every 30 minutes of exercise.

During training and exercise, players like **Dyson Heppell (right)** perspire heavily and lose litres of fluid from their bodies. You can test how well you've kept up your fluids during training or in a match by weighing yourself before and after. If you've lost weight, you haven't drunk enough through the session. And remember, if you're thirsty, you're already in need of a drink.

## QUICK ⑦ QUIZ
What is the weight, in grams of a litre of water?

### DID Y◉U KNOW?
In warm conditions, like those we often see in Queensland, Western Australia and the Northern Territory, a player can lose up to four kilograms during a game. No wonder the water boys and girls are busy at those venues.

The umpire is always right

LAWS OF FOOTY

## ALL ABOUT... THE HALL OF FAME

The Australian Football Hall of Fame was founded in 1996, the year the AFL celebrated its centenary season. It is the one award that rewards the whole of a career, and not just a season. In that first year, 136 players, coaches, administrators, umpires and journalists were inducted into the Hall of Fame. Those initial members of the Hall of Fame traced back to the origins of the game of Australian Football—from 1858—and also included 12 Legends of the game. Legends are the top of the tree in the Hall of Fame—a Legend is a player or coach who has changed the game 'significantly for the better'. In 2018, former Richmond champion, and Essendon and GWS GIANTS coach **Kevin Sheedy (right)** became the 28th Legend.

### QUICK ? QUIZ

The Australian Football Hall of Fame is housed in Australia's most famous ground.

**WHERE IS IT?**

**CLUE:** It's also the home of the Grand Final

### DID Y☺U KNOW?

Admission to the Australian Football Hall of Fame is not just for those who excelled in the VFL or the AFL; it's for those who were champions of their craft in Leagues and Associations across Australia.

# TALKING FOOTY

Hidden in each row of 10 letters are two four-letter words that together form a common footy phrase. Each word reads from left to right and is in sequence, separated by random letters. Each letter can be used only once. The first one has been done for you.

**DEGREE OF DIFFICULTY** ★ ★ ☆

**QUICK ? QUIZ**
Rhyming slang plays a big part in some footy commentators' language.

**WHAT DO THE FOLLOWING PHRASES REFER TO?**

Hey diddle diddle; Sausage roll; Hammer and tack; Mince pies; Froth and bubble.

| F | E | K | R | I | C | L | E | K | E |
|---|---|---|---|---|---|---|---|---|---|

Example: FREE KICK

| D | A | P | R | U | O | N | T | G | P |
|---|---|---|---|---|---|---|---|---|---|

1. __ __ __ __   __ __ __ __

| P | G | N | L | A | A | M | P | E | N |
|---|---|---|---|---|---|---|---|---|---|

2. __ __ __ __   __ __ __ __

| G | B | P | O | O | E | A | L | S | T |
|---|---|---|---|---|---|---|---|---|---|

3. __ __ __ __   __ __ __ __

| S | T | L | E | I | A | S | M | T | E |
|---|---|---|---|---|---|---|---|---|---|

4. __ __ __ __   __ __ __ __

## DID YOU KNOW?

Collingwood has played in a record 44 Grand Finals, (including re-matches), the first in 1901, the most recent in 2018. The Magpies have won 15, second behind Essendon and Carlton for League flags. Their other Grand Final record is not a happy one—27 losses in the decider.

LAWS OF FOOTY

Always stay positive

**EST. 1994**

**FREMANTLE**
# DOCKERS

**ESTABLISHED** 1994

**CAPTAIN** Nat Fyfe

**SENIOR COACH** Justin Longmuir

Fremantle joined the AFL in 1995 as the second team from the West, joining what became their arch rivals, the West Coast Eagles. The Dockers have won over fans across the country with their relentless and tough football. In 2003, the club made history when its 22-man team featured a record seven Indigenous players—Jeff Farmer, Steven Koops, Des Headland, Roger Hayden, Dion Woods, Antoni Grover and **Troy Cook (left)**. The annual Derbies between the two WA clubs get supporters out in full force. Freo has produced champions of the game such as Matthew Pavlich and the current skipper Nat Fyfe. Fyfe won the Brownlow Medal in 2015. In 2017, Fremantle was one of eight clubs chosen to compete in the inaugural AFLW competition, beating out rivals West Coast for a position.

## JOHNNY'S MAGIC MOMENTS

**1** Freo fans went home singing after the Dockers downed the Eagles in round 16, 1999. It was the club's first win against West Coast after nine Derby losses.

**2** In round 21 of 2005 against St Kilda, with the seconds ticking down and behind by just a point, Justin Longmuir launched above the pack to take a huge mark in front of goal. He went back after the siren and put the ball straight through the middle to seal the win for the Dockers.

**3** In 2013, Freo's Preliminary Final victory against Sydney by 25 points was one of the most incredible defensive performances ever witnessed. In front of 43,249 supporters the Dockers stormed into their first Grand Final.

## FROM THE BEGINNING

JOINED THE AFL: 1995
PREMIERSHIPS: 0
GAMES RECORD-HOLDER: Matthew Pavlich (353)
GOALS RECORD-HOLDER: Matthew Pavlich (700)
JOINED THE AFLW: 2017

## CLUB SONG
(BASED IN PART ON THE SONG OF THE VOLGA BOATMEN)

Freo, way to go!
Hit 'em real hard,
send 'em down below
Oh Freo, give 'em the old heave ho
We are the Freo Dockers!

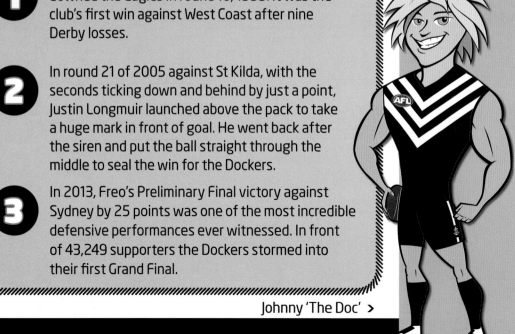

Johnny 'The Doc' >

**JOHNNY'S** ONE TO WATCH

# 7
# NAT FYFE

It would be hard to find a better player in the AFL than Nat Fyfe. One of the most dominant midfielders in the League, it is easy to see why the muscular Fremantle captain has won two Brownlow Medals (2015, 2019), two club best and fairest awards (2013-14) and two All Australian guernseys (2014-15). He's a dead set gun!

## QUICK QUIZ

Fremantle have been minor Premiers once.

### IN WHICH YEAR DID THIS OCCUR?

**CLUE:** They finished with 17 wins, their highest win total in the home and away season.

........................................

ANSWER

........................................

## DID YOU KNOW?

**Matthew Pavlich (below),** the club captain from 2007-2015, was recruited from the Adelaide club, Woodville-West Torrens. He holds the most records at the club: most games (353), most games as captain (190), most best and fairest awards (6), most goals (700), most goals in a season (72), most finals games (15), most All Australian guernseys (6) and most times the leading goalkicker (8).

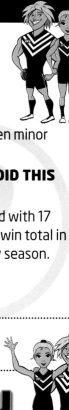

# FREMANTLEFC. COM.AU

**JENNY'S** ONE TO WATCH

# 10
## KIARA BOWERS

As much as any player picked in the 2019 AFLW All Australian team, Kiara Bowers earned her honour through persistence. Due to knee injuries, the Dockers star had to wait on the sidelines for 30 months before her AFLW debut. Her patience was rewarded in 2019—she was named the club's best and fairest player in her spectacular maiden season, edging out Dana Hooker and Gemma Houghton.

**2019 CAPTAIN**
Kara Donnellan

**2020 SENIOR COACH**
Trent Cooper

When the Dockers successfully campaigned for an AFLW licence for the 2017 season, they were unique among applicants: Fremantle would offer all of its players education and job opportunities as well as a game of footy. After a slow start, with one and three wins in their first two seasons, the Dockers charged in 2019, losing only one game in the home and away season before going down to the Blues in the preliminary final.

Jenny >

# FOOTY A TO Z

Use each of the letters of the alphabet—once only—to complete the footy words below. The words relate to players and parts of the game and three words refer to what happens when you kick the ball through the big sticks. Here's a clue to get you started: the four-letter word is the given name of Essendon's best and fairest winner in 2016.

DEGREE OF
DIFFICULTY ★ ★ ☆

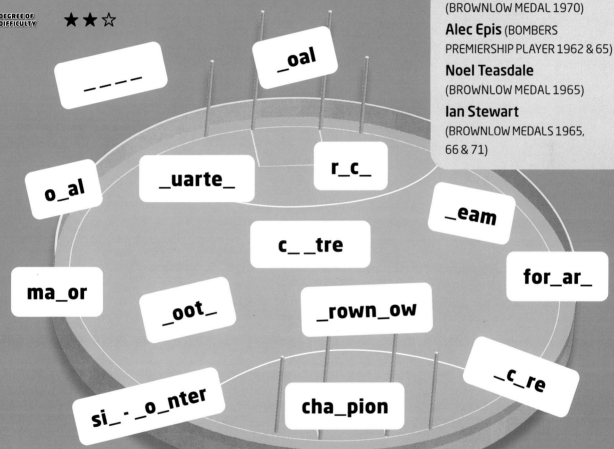

_ _ _ _

_oal

o_al

_uarte_

r_c_

_eam

c_ _tre

for_ar_

ma_or

_oot_

_rown_ow

_c_re

si_ - _o_nter

cha_pion

A B C D E
F G H I J K
L M N O P
Q R S T U
V W X Y Z

## DID Y❀U KNOW?

**Ian Stewart (right)** is one of four people who has won the Brownlow Medal three times. The others are Haydn Bunton (Fitzroy—1931, 1932, 1935), Dick Reynolds (Essendon—1934, 1937, 1938) and Bob Skilton (Swans—1959, 1963, 1968). Stewart won Brownlows while at St Kilda in 1965 and 66 and at Richmond in 1971.

The dominant feature of any footy ground is the ultimate target—**THE GOALPOSTS**. The AFL applies strict rules about the height of the posts and the distance between them. At official AFL grounds the goalposts must be at least 15 metres high and the behind posts 10 metres high. AFL suppliers are Abel Sports and Pila.

At other grounds, they have to be at least 6 metres tall and the behind posts at least 3 metres high. Each post is exactly 6.4 metres apart (this distance was set in the rules written in 1866, as 7 yards; Australia changed to the metric system in 1988).

Do you know who makes goalposts? They're made by flagpole makers, and a set of aluminium goalposts for your ground, delivered and installed, will cost about $4,000. A set for an official AFL ground will cost around $19,000. Since 1964, Law was introduced that padding, (to a minimum height of 2.5 metres for non-AFL venues, and 3 metres at official AFL grounds) must be wrapped around all posts, for the protection of the players. **NO PADDING. NO PLAY.**

## QUICK ⑦ QUIZ

We call it a goalsquare, but it's not a square at all, measuring 9 metres by 6.4 metres. Nobody knows why it has been called a square as it has always been rectangular in shape. From 2019, the player on the mark after a behind is scored must be 10 metres from the top of the square; previously this was 5 metres.

**HOW FAR DOES THE FULL-BACK HAVE TO KICK THE BALL FROM THE EDGE OF THE GOALSQUARE TO FLY OVER THE 50-METRE ARC?**

6.4 metres apart

10 metres high

2-3 metres high

At least 15 metres high in AFL games

9 metres

6.4 metres

6.4 metres apart

## DID Y☺U KNOW?

Hawthorn champion, and Legend of the Australian Hall of Fame, **Leigh Matthews (right)** crashed into a behind post at Essendon's old ground, Windy Hill, in 1982, breaking it in two. No wonder his nickname is 'Lethal'!

# PIE & SAUCE

So, you've got your scarf, beanie, badges, guernsey and your footy *Record*. What else makes a great day out at the footy? Great company, and... a pie & sauce, of course, or a hot dog or a serve of chips. These might not be the healthiest items for a player, but if you're in the crowd you need a different sort of food—comfort food, or food that makes you feel good.

The word **PIE** goes back more than 700 years and there are lots of theories about its origins. One will be loved by Collingwood fans: that PIE is a shortened form of **MAGPIE**, the theory being that a magpie gathers up all sorts of objects, and a pie is often filled with bits and pieces of meat. The word **SAUCE** also comes from way back, as a version of 'salsus', meaning 'salted', from that old language Latin. Footy fans will know that 'sauce' is also the nickname of former Adelaide Crows and now GWS GIANTS ruckman Sam Jacobs.

## QUICK ? QUIZ

Collingwood has always had the nickname 'The Pies'. But Collingwood was formed in 1892 from which other team that played at Victoria Park? **CLUE:** Think of Great Britain.

## DID Y⊚U KNOW?

On Grand Final day at the MCG, fans will eat more than 25,000 pies and sausage rolls, almost 5,000 hot dogs and 25,000 serves of hot chips.

# GEELONG CATS

**ESTABLISHED** 1859

**CAPTAIN** Joel Selwood

**SENIOR COACH** Chris Scott

Geelong is the only AFL team based in a provincial city, and it receives huge support from the local community. It has been that way for a long time, as the Cats are the second oldest football club (behind Melbourne) in Australia, founded in 1859. The Cats have been one of the most dominant teams in the modern era, winning flags in 2007, 2009 and 2011. They have produced some absolute champions of the game including the famous Ablett family—Gary Ablett Snr and his sons Gary Jnr and Nathan. Geelong produced the first winner of the Brownlow Medal (named after a former Geelong captain, Charles Brownlow), in **'Carji' Greeves (left)**, and has since had six more, the most recent being Patrick Dangerfield in 2016. The Cats also fielded their first AFLW team in 2019.

## FROM THE BEGINNING

CLUB FORMED: 1859
JOINED THE VFL/AFL: 1897
PREMIERSHIPS: 9 -
1925, 1931, 1937,
1951-1952, 1963,
2007, 2009, 2011
GAMES RECORD-HOLDER:
Corey Enright (332)
GOALS RECORD-HOLDER:
Gary Ablett Snr (1021)
JOINED THE AFLW: 2019

## CLUB SONG

(TO THE TUNE OF THE TOREADOR SONG BY BIZET)

We are Geelong,
the greatest team of all
We are Geelong,
we're always on the ball
We play the game as
it should be played
At home or far away
Our banners fly high from
dawn to dark
Down at Kardinia
Park

## HALF CAT'S MAGIC MOMENTS

**1** Geelong holds the record for the most wins in a row: 23, from round 12, 1952 to round 13, 1953. That streak included a 46-point victory over Collingwood in the Grand Final.

**2** In round 6, 1993, Gary Ablett kicked 14.7 against Essendon at the MCG. But guess what? The Cats still lost! It is the biggest goal tally by a player in a losing side. In that same game, Paul Salmon kicked 10 goals for the Bombers!

**3** Geelong holds the record for the biggest margin in a Grand Final, beating Port Adelaide by 119 points in 2007. It was the sweetest victory, breaking a Premiership drought of 34 years.

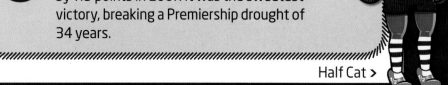

Half Cat >

HALF CAT'S ONE TO WATCH

# 5 PATRICK DANGERFIELD

Danger! There isn't a more explosive and exciting player in the game than Patrick Dangerfield. No other player can match his ability to break through a pack at blistering speed. Already one of the game's greats, Danger moved back home to Geelong from Adelaide, and has packed his trophy cabinet with every award in the book. As well as his Brownlow Medal, he's a seven-time All Australian, has won three club best and fairest awards (two at Geelong, one at Adelaide) and also bagged a Players' Association player of the year award.

## QUICK QUIZ

**Gary Ablett senior (right)** holds the Geelong club record for goals kicked (1,021), but he also kicked 10 goals at another club, at which his brothers Kevin and Geoff also played.

**WHAT WAS HIS FIRST LEAGUE CLUB?**

........................................................

**ANSWER**

........................................................

## DID YOU KNOW?

**Jimmy Bartel (below)**, Geelong's 2007 Brownlow Medallist, holds the record for the most consecutive wins at an AFL venue. From round 7, 2007 to round 20, 2011, Bartel played in 33 games at Kardinia Park, Geelong's home ground, without losing a match.

# GEELONGCATS .COM.AU

GEELONG CATS

2019
CAPTAIN
Melissa
Hickey

2020
SENIOR
COACH
Paul Hood

# 18
## MELISSA HICKEY

Footy is in Melissa Hickey's blood. Her great, great-uncle, Pat Hickey, played in the very first round of VFL football in 1897, and her grandfather's cousin, Reg Hickey, was a legend at Geelong. After a two-season stint with Melbourne, Melissa Hickey was named Geelong's inaugural AFLW captain in 2019. A seven-time VFLW premiership player and All Australian in 2017, she's a star for the Cats!

Although the Cats were foundation members of the AFL in 1897, and one of the game's earliest clubs (founded in 1859), they had to wait two years to make their AFLW debut during the 2019 season. It was worth the wait: the Cats finished second in Conference B to make the finals in their inaugural year. The likes of Melissa Hickey, Meg McDonald and Maddy McMahon will have them challenging again in 2020.

Clawdia >

**ALL ABOUT...** SCORES

The highest winning **SCORE** in AFL history was kicked by Geelong against Brisbane in round 7, 1992. The Cats kicked 37.17 (239) to Brisbane's 11.9 (75). This was one point more than Fitzroy's 36.22 (238) to Melbourne's 6.12 (48) in round 17, 1979. However, that effort earned Fitzroy the record for greatest winning margin. The lowest score is St Kilda's one behind to Geelong's 23.24 (162) in round 17, 1899. The lowest winning score is Essendon's 1.8 (14) against Melbourne 0.8 (8), and that was in the 1897 Grand Final. The highest score in a quarter belongs to the Swans, set in round 12, 1919, when they scored 17.4 (106) in the last quarter against St Kilda. The biggest comeback was in round 16, 2001, when Essendon came from 69 points behind the Roos at the 10-minute mark of the second quarter. The Bombers eventually won by 12 points—27.9 (171) to 25.9 (159).

### QUICK QUIZ

How many points did Geelong win by when it set the record against Brisbane in 1992?

### DID YOU KNOW?

Hawthorn holds a record that may never be broken. In round 6, 1977, the Hawks kicked 25.41 (191) to beat St Kilda 16.7 (103). That behinds tally of 41 is the most kicked by a club in any AFL match, and 66 is the most shots for goal, beating Carlton's 60 shots against Hawthorn in round 2, 1969—30.30 (120) to 12.10 (82). Two Hawks, Don Scott and Peter Hudson, played in both of those games!

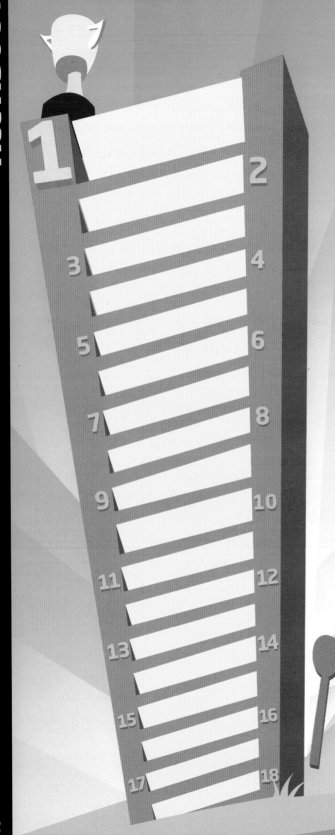

The AFL ladder—sometimes called the AFL table—might be the most viewed set of numbers that any footy fan will watch throughout the season. The basics are easy to understand. Winning teams get 4 points for a win, 2 points for a draw and none for a loss. Where it gets complicated is the way the AFL separates teams that have the same number of points: that's decided by what's called *percentage*. Percentage is worked out by dividing the points scored by the points against, the result multiplied by 100. So, if, in round 1, your team wins, with 120 points against 60 points, the percentage is (120/60) x 100=200. Wouldn't that be nice! At the end of the 2018 season, Melbourne and Sydney both had 14 wins, and 56 points, but Melbourne had the greater percentage, which meant the Demons finished fifth and the Swans sixth. In 2017, Melbourne missed a place in the final eight by just 0.49 per cent; all the Demons needed to do was kick 11 points more, and they would have replaced the Eagles.

### QUICK ⑦ QUIZ

In 2000, Essendon lost only one game in the 22-round home and away season.

**HOW MANY POINTS DID THE BOMBERS HAVE ON THE LADDER AT THE END OF THE SEASON?**

### DID Y⊛U KNOW?

The highest percentage was gathered by Collingwood in 1902, when the Magpies finished the season with 15 wins and a percentage of 199.46. The Pies went on to beat Essendon in the Grand Final.

# BRAINBUSTER

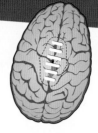

At the end of the season, three footballers each decide to play a practical joke on the club's football manager, physio and social club manager. From the clues below, can you work out which player played a trick on which staff member and what was that person's job at the club?

**DEGREE OF DIFFICULTY**  ★ ★ ★

## CLUES

The players' names are JASON, BRAD and SHANE (you can write those down in any order in the answer box) and their surnames, not necessarily in the same order, are JONES, SMITH and CARTER. The staff members' names are Ms JOHNSON, Ms DERUM and Mr BROWN.

1. Jason played his practical joke on the female physio.
2. Jones played his practical joke on Ms Derum.
3. The football manager was caught out by Smith's practical joke.
4. Brad did not play his joke on Mr Brown and Shane did not play his joke on the social club manager, who is not Ms Johnson.

| FIRST NAME | SURNAME | STAFF NAME | POSITION |
|---|---|---|---|
|  |  |  |  |
|  |  |  |  |
|  |  |  |  |

Meet every challenge head on

# SUNS

| | |
|---|---|
| **ESTABLISHED** | 2009 |
| **CAPTAINS** | David Swallow & Jarrod Witts |
| **SENIOR COACH** | Stuart Dew |

The Gold Coast SUNS are the second newest team to enter the AFL, and the second team based in Queensland. The club's first captain was Gary Ablett Jnr, a superstar of the League. He won a Brownlow Medal in 2013, matching his 2009 Medal while at Geelong. The young SUNS showed signs of improvement in 2013, finishing with eight wins, and then in 2014 started the season with seven wins and only two losses. They were looking to make their first finals appearance but they could win only one game after Gary Ablett went down with a shoulder injury in round 16. Since that moment, the SUNS have struggled, as indicated by their four coaches in just eight seasons. Here's hoping Stuart Dew leads them into a new era! The SUNS are also set to join the AFLW in the 2020 season.

## SUNNY RAY'S MAGIC MOMENTS

**1** In round 5 of the 2011 season, the SUNS recorded their first win in the AFL against Port Adelaide. Despite trailing by 23 points at half-time, they kicked 10 of the last 16 goals to win narrowly at Football Park in Adelaide.

**2** Gold Coast's two highest scores have been against the other newcomer to the AFL competition, GWS GIANTS—21.22 (148) and 22.14 (146). The SUNS won 4 out of 5 of their first games against the GIANTS, but have not beaten them since round 6, 2014.

**3** After 11 straight losses, the SUNS shocked the footy world with a comeback victory over Sydney at the SCG in round 18, 2018. The Swans kicked the first 5 goals of the match and led by 29 points at quarter-time, but could manage just 2 more goals after the first break, as the SUNS piled on 11.11 to win by 24 points.

Sunny Ray >

## FROM THE BEGINNING

JOINED THE AFL: 2011
PREMIERSHIPS: 0
GAMES RECORD HOLDER: Jarrod Harbrow (175)
GOALS RECORD HOLDER: Tom Lynch (254)
JOINING THE AFLW: 2020

## CLUB SONG
(IN SING-A-LONG STYLE)

We are the SUNS of the Gold Coast sky
We are the one in the red, gold and blue
We are the mighty Gold Coast SUNS
We play to win the flag for you. Fight! Fight! Fight!
Till we hold up the cup
Run run run all the way
We are the SUNS of the Gold Coast sky
We're the team who never say die

# 24
# DAVID SWALLOW

David Swallow was the No.1 pick in the 2010 NAB AFL Draft. He has been a consistent performer for the SUNS, especially when the chips are down. In 2014 he showed his quality, breaking Gary Ablett Jnr's run of best and fairest wins. Although injuries have been constant for Swallow, his beautiful skills and speed through the middle make him a formidable opponent for any midfielder.

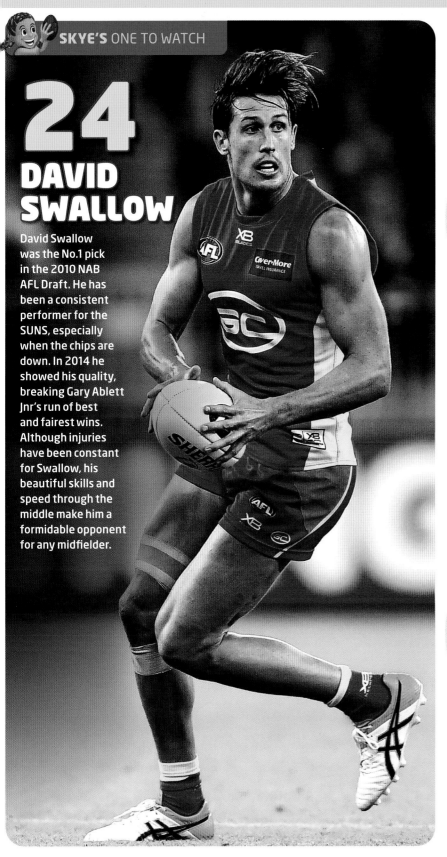

Skye >

## QUICK QUIZ

Gold Coast's first game in the AFL was against Carlton at the Gabba.

**WHILE THE RESULT DIDN'T GO THE SUNS' WAY, WHO KICKED THE FIRST GOAL FOR THE CLUB?**

**CLUE:** He now plays for the Power.

.................................................

**ANSWER**

.................................................

## DID YOU KNOW?

Although the SUNS only entered the AFL in 2011, it took just three seasons before the club had its first Brownlow Medallist—**Gary Ablett Jnr (right)** in 2013. Ablett was also club champion in the SUNS' first three years, and again in his final season, 2017—as well as leading their goal kicking in both 2012 and 2013—exceptional work for a midfielder!

# GOLDCOASTFC .COM.AU

CLUB ZONE

# PERFECT PAIR

Two of the four spider webs—no, they're not named after the 'Spiders' of footy, like Peter Everitt, Matthew Burton or Aaron Sandilands!—are the same. Can you find them? You might want to turn the page around.

DEGREE OF DIFFICULTY ★ ★ ★

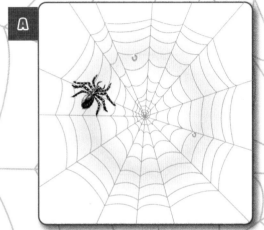

A

B

C

D

## DID YOU KNOW?

Since League footy started in 1897, 21 sets of twins either have played or are playing the game. In 2019, there is only one set—Jake and Kade Kolodjashnij, who play for Geelong and Melbourne respectively. Soon to join them are the King twins—Max at St Kilda and Ben at Gold Coast—and although Nathan Brown is still playing for the Saints, his twin brother, Mitch, finished up at the Eagles after the 2016 season.

## ALL ABOUT... TALLEST & SHORTEST

**QUICK ⑦ QUIZ**

What is the height difference between Mason Cox and Caleb Daniel?

**F**ooty is a game for all shapes and sizes and, as coaching legend David Parkin once said, for both **TALLS AND SMALLS**. Western Bulldog Caleb Daniel is the shortest player in the AFL in 2019 at 168 centimetres, making him the shortest player in the League since fellow Bulldog and 1990 Brownlow Medallist Tony Liberatore, who was 163 centimetres. At the other end of the scale, at 211 centimetres, Collingwood's Mason Cox towers over most people he meets as the tallest current player. Fremantle champion Aaron Sandilands and former Cat and Bulldog Peter Street were the same height as Cox—the all-time AFL record. Although accurate tallies weren't always kept in the past, many believe that Collingwood and North Melbourne forward Jim 'Nipper' Bradford was the shortest player in League history at 155 centimetres. Bradford played 16 League games and, at 53 kilograms, also earned the distinction of being the second-lightest player to take an AFL field. Essendon's George Shorten—nickname Titch—was only 163 centimetres tall and weighed 51 kilograms, and finished equal second in 1924's inaugural Brownlow Medal voting!

**TALL TIMBER:** At 211cm, Collingwood's American import Mason Cox is a giant of the competition—especially next to Bulldog Caleb Daniel, who stands just 168cm tall.

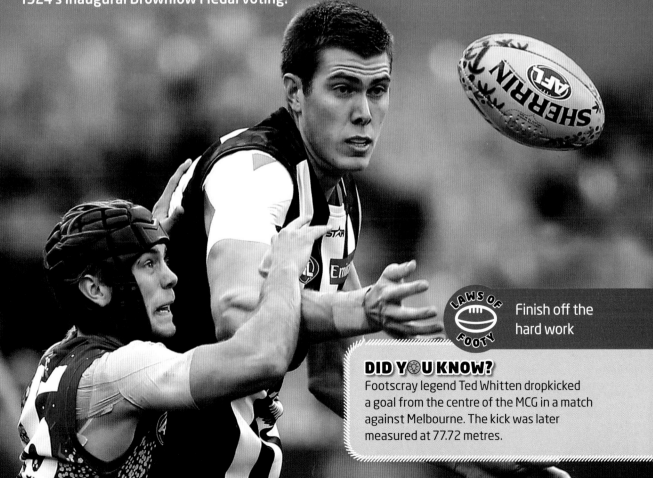

**LAWS OF FOOTY**

Finish off the hard work

**DID YOU KNOW?**
Footscray legend Ted Whitten dropkicked a goal from the centre of the MCG in a match against Melbourne. The kick was later measured at 77.72 metres.

# GIANTS

**ESTABLISHED** 2010

**CAPTAIN** Stephen Conigio

**SENIOR COACH** Leon Cameron

The GWS GIANTS found their opening four years difficult at AFL level, collecting two wooden spoons, while showing flashes of what was to come. Success eventually came in 2016 when the GIANTS shot up the ladder from 11th in 2015, finishing the season in the top four but losing the Preliminary Final to the eventual Premiers, the Western Bulldogs. They did the same the following season, losing the preliminary final, again to the Premiers, Richmond. In 2019, the GIANTS overcame injuries to key players, and made it to their first Grand Final, after winning three thrilling finals. The GIANTS are setting new membership records each year, and were also a part of the first season of the AFLW in 2017.

**TOUGH:** GIANTS captain Amanda Farrugia is one of the bravest midfielders in the AFLW.

## G-MAN'S MAGIC MOMENTS

1. The GIANTS, coached by the great Kevin Sheedy, entered the AFL competition in 2012, playing their opening game against the Swans.
2. The GIANTS would have to wait until round 7 in their first season to get their first win, against fellow newcomers the Gold Coast SUNS.
3. The club's great leap forward came in 2016, when the GIANTS notched up 16 wins and finished fourth. After winning just 9 games in their first 3 seasons, the GIANTS won 54 (plus three draws) in seasons 2015-18.

GMAN >

## FROM THE BEGINNING

**JOINED THE AFL:** 2012
**PREMIERSHIPS:** 0
**GAMES RECORD HOLDER:** Callan Ward (157)
**GOALS RECORD HOLDER:** Jeremy Cameron (403)
**JOINED THE AFLW:** 2017

## CLUB SONG

Well there's a big, big sound
From the West of the town
It's the sound of the mighty
GIANTS
You feel the ground A-SHAKING
The other teams are quaking
In their boots before the GIANTS
We take the longest strides
And the highest leap
We're stronger than the rest
We're the Greater Western
Sydney GIANTS
We're the biggest and the best
And we will never surrender
We'll fight until the end
We're greater than the rest

GMAN'S ONE TO WATCH

# 22
# JOSH KELLY

If you see Josh Kelly tearing through the middle of the ground and delivering the perfect pass, you might wonder where his talent comes from. Kelly's father, Phil, was a champion in his own right, winning two Sandover Medals (best and fairest in the WA Footy League) at East Perth before playing 61 games for North Melbourne. Like his dad, Josh Kelly can run all day—so much so that the Roos offered him big bucks to join them when his contract with GWS GIANTS was over! He stuck with the GIANTS, where he won the Kevin Sheedy Medal in 2017, the same year he won All Australian honours. Past the 100-game mark now for the GIANTS, Josh Kelly's star rises with every passing week. He's a son of a gun!

## QUICK QUIZ

In the club's eight seasons, one person has been at the top of the goalkicking table every year.

**WHO IS HE?**

**CLUE:** He shares his last name with the club's coach.

ANSWER

## DID YOU KNOW?

The GIANTS already have two life members of the club. One is Kevin Sheedy, the club's inaugural coach, and the other is co-captain Callan Ward. The GIANTS also honoured Sheedy by naming their best and fairest trophy the Kevin Sheedy Medal.

# GWSGIANTS.COM.AU

# GWS GIANTS

**GIGI'S** ONE TO WATCH

# 24
# HANEEN ZREIKA

A zippy midfielder who sometimes switches to defence, 157cm pocket rocket Haneen Zreika burst onto the AFLW scene in 2019. Perhaps it's her Rugby League background that makes her so adept at dodging and weaving. When Zreika made her debut, she was looking forward to two things: getting her first kick and making history as the first Muslim woman to play AFLW.

**2019 CAPTAIN**
Amanda Farrugia

**2020 SENIOR COACH**
Alan McConnell

Like the GIANTS' men's team, it's been a slow build for the Greater Western Sydney AFLW team. One win in their first year was followed by three in their second. Inspirational captain Amanda Farrugia, Alyce Parker and Rebecca Beeson were the stars in 2019, and the future looks bright for the women of Sydney's west.

CLUB ZONE

GIGI >

**ALL ABOUT...** THE LONGEST KICK

**QUICK ? QUIZ**
How many AFL clubs has Malcolm Blight coached, for how many Premierships?

**LAWS OF FOOTY**
Practise kicking with both the left and right foot from the beginning

**DID YOU KNOW?**
If the man on the mark is in the middle of the centre circle at the MCG, they would have to kick more than 80 metres to clear the goal-line.

**HEAVE HO:**
Jonathon Patton came to the GWS GIANTS as the number one pick in the 2011 AFL National Draft and played 89 games before leaving the GIANTS to join the Hawks in 2020. He is no stranger to roosting the ball high and long, and set an AFL record for the longest goal in 2016.

When people start discussing the LONGEST KICKS in footy, the truth is often lost in the telling. Old-timers reckon the longest kick of all time was measured in 1899, when Essendon's Albert Thurgood booted the footy 98.48 metres at training. Given that, in those days, players only trained once or twice a week, and were nowhere near as strong as the modern player, we doubt that tale. Since TV was introduced in 1956, there are examples of long kicks that can be measured, including a monster from Legend of the game Malcolm Blight, whose goal after the siren has been measured at 83 metres. Since 2013, the AFL's official statistician, Champion Data, has been measuring shots for goal: their leader is Jonathon Patton, who goaled from 73 metres against Sydney in round 3, 2016, when playing for the GWS GIANTS. In the last three years, Fox Footy has conducted a long kick contest on Grand Final day: the best kick recorded is by Carlton's Bryce Gibbs—72.3 metres in 2016.

## ALL ABOUT... SUPPORTING A CLUB

**C**lubs are the life-blood of footy, at all levels—from AFL Auskick through juniors to the AFL. There is something very special about **SUPPORTING YOUR CLUB**—you become part of a big family. At the AFL, for a few hours every weekend, complete strangers become pals, as they cheer on their team from the sidelines. In 2019, membership of AFL clubs rose to a record 1,057,572.

The same passion applies at every level of the game. Have you been to a match in the bush, when fans drive their cars around the ground, tooting horns at great moments of play? It's a great experience. Often fans become part of the club, as members, or as volunteers, helping out at every level, from cutting up oranges, to managing the club.

Singing your club's theme song after a win is one of the great things about footy.

**MANY OF THE AFL SONGS ALSO END UP FORMING THE SONG OF JUNIOR CLUBS, BUT WHICH TEAM SONG, IN ITS ORIGINAL FORM, WAS PERFORMED BY ROCK STARS LIKE THE BEATLES AND ELVIS PRESLEY?**

**CLUE:** It's a marching song.

Go hard at every contest

LAWS OF FOOTY

### DID Y⚽U KNOW?

All players who make it to the AFL have been fans of clubs before they started their career, but not all of them end up at the club they loved before they were drafted. For example, two-time Norm Smith Medallist, Luke Hodge, was a fan of the Tigers, before joining the Hawks in 2001. In 2017, he moved to Brisbane, to become an on-field teacher, as well as an important part of the Lions' defence.

## ALL ABOUT... THE MARVEL STADIUM ROOF

When **MARVEL STADIUM**, at Melbourne's Docklands, was added as an official playing venue in 2000, the AFL had to introduce a new rule to account for the stadium's retractable roof! There is now a Law to cover the unlikely event of the footy hitting the roof, but a free kick is to be paid only if the offending player does it on purpose. The roof is between 32 metres (at the boundary line) and 38 metres above the ground, so you'd have to be reckless— and have a super boot—to kick the ball at the roof on purpose. If it happens by accident, the umpire will bounce the ball, or throw it up. Not surprisingly, the footy hasn't yet hit the roof, by any means, during an AFL match. More about the roof: it's made of about 4,000 tonnes of steel; it consists of two panels measuring 165 by 50 metres; the longest single span is 150 metres; it can open or close in 20 minutes; instead of light towers, there are 740 individual 2,000-watt lights under the rim of the roof.

Work hard to achieve your goals

LAWS OF FOOTY

### QUICK ? QUIZ

The light bulbs used in homes are generally between 40 and 100 watts.

**HOW MANY 40-WATT BULBS WOULD YOU NEED TO PRODUCE THE SAME LIGHT AS ONE OF MARVEL STADIUM'S 2,000-WATT BULBS?**

### DID YOU KNOW?

A 600-tonne crane had to be specially imported from Germany to erect Marvel Stadium's retractable roof.

# HAWKS

| | |
|---|---|
| **ESTABLISHED** 1902 | |
| **CAPTAIN** Ben Stratton | |
| **SENIOR COACH** Alastair Clarkson | |

Since joining the League in 1925, Hawthorn has had five 'home' grounds—Glenferrie Oval in Hawthorn, Princes Park in North Carlton, VFL Park/Waverley Park in Waverley, the MCG in Jolimont, and University of Tasmania Stadium in Launceston. The club mixes its 'home' games between the MCG and Launceston. Hawthorn was known as the Mayblooms until 1942, when legendary coach Roy Cazaly decided the Hawks was a more fitting name. 'C'arn the Hawks!' has been the club's catch cry ever since. The Hawks have had their fair share of champions, but none greater than 'Lethal' Leigh Matthews. He was as tough and as skilled as they come, winning a club record eight best and fairest awards. Michael Tuck captained the Hawks to four Premierships (1986, 88, 89, 91) and holds the League record for finals played (39), final wins (26), and Premierships won (7). Peter Hudson shares the game's goal-kicking record for a season with the Swans' Bob Pratt (150). Recently, coached by Alastair Clarkson, the Hawks have become one of greatest teams of all, winning three Premierships in a row from 2013-2015, along with 2008. Only four coaches—Jock McHale (8), Norm Smith (6), John Worrall (5) and Frank Hughes (5)—have coached more Premierships than Clarkson.

### HAWKA'S MAGIC MOMENTS

**1** On the last Saturday in September 1961, Hawthorn won its first Premiership, 36 years after joining the VFL along with Footscray and North Melbourne.

**2** Against the heavily favoured Geelong in the 2008 Grand Final, Hawthorn came from nowhere to win by 26-points, with club legend Luke Hodge winning the first of his two Norm Smith medals.

**3** Hawthorn completed a three-peat of Premierships in 2015, a feat only Carlton, Collingwood, Melbourne (twice) and Brisbane have been able to equal in the history of the League.

Hawka >

---

# FROM THE BEGINNING

**CLUB FORMED:** 1902
**JOINED THE VFL/AFL:** 1925
**PREMIERSHIPS WON: 13 -** 1961, 1971, 1976, 1978, 1983, 1986, 1988-89, 1991, 2008, 2013, 2014, 2015
**GAMES RECORD-HOLDER:** Michael Tuck (426)
**GOALS RECORD-HOLDER:** Jason Dunstall (1,254)

# CLUB SONG

## (TO THE TUNE OF YANKEE DOODLE DANDY)

We're a happy team at Hawthorn
We're the mighty fighting Hawks
We love our club and we play to win
Riding the bumps with a grin (at Hawthorn)
Come what may, you'll find us striving
Teamwork is the thing that talks
One for all and all for one
Is the way we play at Hawthorn
We are the Mighty Fighting Hawks

**HAWKETTE'S** ONE TO WATCH

# 10
## JAEGER O'MEARA

Jaeger O'Meara joined Hawthorn in 2017 after four years at Gold Coast, where he won the 2013 Rising Star award in his first AFL season. After missing nearly three full seasons with knee injuries, the handsome Hawk returned in style in 2018, and is now a star of Hawthorn's midfield. When the ball is there to be had, the Western Australian running machine often ends up with it.

# QUICK QUIZ

Hawthorn holds the League record for most behinds kicked in a game—41 against St Kilda in 1977. The Hawks had a total score of 191 points that day.

**CAN YOU WORK OUT HOW MANY GOALS THEY KICKED?**

......................................

ANSWER

......................................

# DID YOU KNOW?

Hawthorn leads the way with Premierships won since the AFL was created in 1990, with five flags—1991, 2008, 2013-15. West Coast is next with four. Since the Hawks won their first flag in 1961, they have won 13—the next best in that era is Carlton with eight.

**WINNING WAYS:** Jack Gunston with the 2015 Premiership Cup

# HAWTHORNFC. COM.AU

FOOD & FITNESS

# FOOTY SKILLS

**A**FL footballers constantly work on their fitness, their strength and their skills. The facilities available to players at all clubs are now world class, and coaches and fitness advisers are there to ensure that each player works to a program that suits their size and shape. Each session is worked out in detail by the coaches, and, as well as skills being practised, so too is the game plan. Clubs often have 'closed sessions' when they wish to work on a specific part of their plan, perhaps around stoppages, or kick-ins, or when protecting a narrow lead near the end of a quarter or a game.

## DID YU KNOW?

Hawthorn midfielder Tom Mitchell is not known as a 'ball magnet' for nothing. In 2018 he set a new record for disposals over the season with 848 in his 24 games; and twice he gathered more than 50 disposals in a match. AFL statistics have been kept since 1965. In that time, Richmond Legend Kevin Bartlett leads the most kicks (634), and former St Kilda champion Nick Riewoldt the most marks (256). Peter Hudson (1971) and Bob Pratt (1934) hold the season record for goals kicked (150).

**HARD WORK:** It's no mistake that Tom Mitchell (left) always hits the target. Like all the best players, he works hard on his skills.

## QUICK ? QUIZ

Which former Geelong and GWS GIANTS forward invented the kick around the corner when shooting for goals?

**CLUE:** He won the Norm Smith Medal in 2007.

## ALL ABOUT... NORM SMITH MEDAL

**W**inning a Premiership Medal is every player's dream, but imagine if you were then voted best player on the ground, and added the Norm Smith Medal to your trophy cabinet! This Medal, named after the Australian Football Hall of Fame Legend, has been presented on Grand Final day since 1979, when Carlton's Wayne Harmes was honoured. So who was Norm Smith? Well, not only was he a champion full-forward, and a member of FOUR Melbourne premiership teams (1939, 1940, 1941, 1948), he was named the Coach of the Century in 1996, after coaching Melbourne to six premierships (1955, 1956, 1957, 1959, 1960, 1964).

Four players have won the Medal twice: Gary Ayres (Hawthorn, 1986, 1988), Andrew McLeod (Adelaide 1997, 1998), Luke Hodge (Hawthorn, 2008, 2014), and Dustin Martin (Richmond, 2017, 2019). Martin is the only player to have won the Brownlow Medal and the Norm Smith Medal in the same year. In 2010, when Collingwood and St Kilda played a draw, there were two winners: Lenny Hayes (Saints, in the first Grand Final), and Scott Pendlebury (Magpies, in the replay). That was the last Grand Final to have a replay in the event of a draw; the AFL changed the rules, and if there's a draw in future, the teams will play two extra periods of five minutes. If the scores are still tied, the first team to score will be the winner.

### DID Y🏉U KNOW?

The first premiership was won by Essendon, in 1897. The Bombers did not play a Grand Final to win the flag: in that first season, the top four teams (Geelong, Essendon, Melbourne and Collingwood), played each other once in a round-robin series. Essendon was the only undefeated team and was declared Premiers. Up to, and including 2018's West Coast team, 1,529 players have played in at least one Premiership team.

### QUICK ❓ QUIZ

What do these Norm Smith Medallists have in common: Tony Shaw (Collingwood, 1990), James Hird (Essendon, 2000), Nathan Buckley (Collingwood, 2002), Chris Judd (West Coast, 2005), and Luke Hodge (Hawthorn, 2014)?

**DUAL NORM SMITH MEDALLIST:**
Luke Hodge won the award in 2008 and 2014.

Always back up your teammates

**ALL ABOUT...** THE BROWNLOW MEDAL

The **BROWNLOW MEDAL** is Australian football's most famous and most coveted individual award. It was created by the League in 1924, to commemorate one of the famous players and administrators of the earliest days of footy, Geelong's **Charles Brownlow (top right)**. The first Brownlow Medal, awarded to the fairest and best player of the season, was won by Geelong centreman Edward Greeves, whose nickname was 'Carji'. Since the beginning, votes for each match are cast by the field umpires—in the first seven seasons only one vote per game was made, but from 1931, the umpires vote on a 3-2-1 basis. Four players have won the Medal three times—Essendon's Dick Reynolds, Fitzroy's Haydn Bunton, Swan Bob Skilton, and Ian Stewart, who won two at St Kilda and one at Richmond. The other individual award is the AFL Players Association's Most Valuable Player award—named after the champion Hawk Leigh Matthews, since 2002. The MVP began in 1982—Matthews was the first winner—and is voted on by all the players.

**BIG NIGHT:** Tom Mitchell joined Hawthorn from Sydney in 2017 and became an instant star with his uncanny ability to find the footy. He won club best and fairest awards in 2017 and 2018, and in 2018 added the Brownlow Medal to his trophy collection. Mitchell missed all of the 2019 season after suffering a broken leg in the pre-season. He returns in 2020 fully fit after a long period of recuperation.

**A**t the inception of the AFLW competition, the League also introduced a Brownlow Medal equivalent for the women's game. **THE NAB AFL WOMEN'S BEST & FAIREST TROPHY** is awarded by the officiating umpires, who award votes on a 3,2,1 basis after each match, with votes to be counted as part of the W Awards. As is the case for the Brownlow, any player suspended by the AFL during the season will be ineligible to receive the award.

The inaugural award of 2017 was won by Adelaide Crow's superstar co-captain Erin Phillips, who also took it home in 2019. Between those triumphs, Western Bulldogs champion Emma Kearney took out the 2018 award. Phillips's 2019 was the most impressive of all—she polled 19 of a possible 21 votes throughout the season, and was awarded full votes for four games. Phillips was also honoured with the AFLW Coaches' Award and AFLW Most Valuable Player Award, a peer voted prize that reflects her standing in the competition.

**LAWS OF FOOTY** Challenge yourself in order to grow

DECORATED: Erin Phillips of Adelaide took out the 2019 AFLW Best and Fairest award, and Carlton's Madison Prespakis (right) the NAB AFL Rising Star award.

**DID YOU KNOW?**
In 2019, Geelong and Gold Coast SUNS champion Gary Ablett Jnr became the highest-polling player in Brownlow Medal history. At the end of the 2019 season, he had gained 261 votes, with an average per game of 0.81 votes. Geelong is also the club with the most votes, ahead of Collingwood and Carlton.

## MELBOURNE

| ESTABLISHED | 1858 |
| --- | --- |
| 2019 CAPTAINS | Nathan Jones & Jack Viney |
| SENIOR COACH | Simon Goodwin |

The history of the Melbourne Football Club dates back almost as far as the birth of the game itself. There's mention of the Melbourne Footy Club in 1859, when the man who wrote the first set of Australian Football rules helped form the club. Once known as the Redlegs or Fuchsias, Melbourne was one of eight original VFL clubs in 1897, but didn't enjoy much success in the first 40 years. After adopting the nickname the Demons in 1933, Melbourne won flags in 1939, 40 and 41. Under coach **Norm Smith (left)**, Melbourne then won a remarkable five flags in six years between 1955 and 1960. The Demons contested Grand Finals in 1988 and 2000, but the club's most recent premiership was in 1964. The Dees were a foundation team of the AFLW in 2017.

### CHUCK'S MAGIC MOMENTS

**1** Melbourne completed a remarkable run of five premierships in six years—1958 was the one that got away—when the Dees thrashed Collingwood by 8 goals in the 1960 Grand Final.

**2** Full-forward Fred Fanning kicked 18 goals against St Kilda in the final round of the 1947 season. It's the most goals kicked by a player in an AFL game.

**3** Irish recruit Jim Stynes won the 1991 Brownlow Medal. What an emotional night that was for big Jim and his dad Brian, who'd flown out from Ireland for the night. The late Demon ruckman went on to play 264 games, including an AFL record 244 in a row!

## FROM THE BEGINNING

CLUB FORMED: 1858
JOINED THE VFL/AFL: 1897
PREMIERSHIPS: **12** - 1900, 1926, 1939-41, 1948, 1955-57, 1959-60, 1964
GAMES RECORD-HOLDER: David Neitz (306)
GOALS RECORD-HOLDER: David Neitz (631)
JOINED THE AFLW: 2017

## CLUB SONG

(TO THE TUNE OF A GRAND OLD FLAG)

It's a grand old flag,
it's a high-flying flag
It's the emblem for me and for you
It's the emblem of the team we love
The team of the RED AND THE BLUE
Every heart beats true for the red and the blue
As we sing this song to you
Should old acquaintance be forgot
Keep your eye on the red and the blue

Chuck >

# 13
# CLAYTON OLIVER

Every time Melbourne surges forward, it seems that Clayton Oliver is heavily involved. In four years at the top level, the Dees midfielder has justified his hyped arrival as the fourth pick in the 2015 National Draft. A Demons best and fairest winner in 2017 and an All Australian in 2018, he's the midfielder who could drive Melbourne towards its first premiership since 1964.

# QUICK QUIZ

Only one man, Jock McHale, has coached more AFL premierships than this member of the Australian Football Hall of Fame. He steered the Dees to flags in 1955, 56, 57, 59, 60 and 64, and is recognised as one of the most innovative coaches ever.

## WHO WAS THIS VERY FAMOUS DEMONS COACH?

**CLUE:** The player judged to be best afield in the AFL Grand Final wins the medal bearing his name.

......................................
ANSWER

# DID YOU KNOW?

One of the most skilful players of his time, Melbourne wingman Robert Flower played 269 games over 15 years before running out in his first final in 1987. The Demon skipper guided his side to huge victories over the Kangaroos and the Swans before a heartbreaking two-point loss to Hawthorn in the preliminary final. Robbie decided to retire after that loss.

# MELBOURNEFC .COM.AU

DAISY'S ONE TO WATCH

## 6
## DAISY PEARCE

There are overachievers and then there is Daisy Pearce. The Melbourne star, who captained the Dees for their first two AFLW seasons, is not only a champion of the game, but, as a respected broadcaster, also the face and voice of women's footy. An All Australian in 2017 and 2018 (she was captain in 2017), somehow she's also managed to find time to have twin babies—a girl, Sylvie, and a boy, Roy. Here's hoping The Demons may have a couple more champions waiting in the wings!

**2019 CAPTAINS**
Elise O'Dea & Shelley Scott

**2020 SENIOR COACH**
Mick Stinear

Along with the Bulldogs, Melbourne was an early supporter of women's football. The Dees fielded their first team for the 2013 exhibition match against the Bulldogs at the MCG, so it was natural they'd join the expanded League in 2017. Melbourne's stars have been Daisy Pearce, Tegan Cunningham, and 2019 best and fairest winner Karen Paxman. The Dees are always hard to beat!

Daisy >

## ALL ABOUT... INTERNATIONAL RULES

There are some amazing similarities between Australian Rules and Ireland's Gaelic football. Did you know that about 100 years ago, Gaelic footy had behind posts? Back in the 1960s, a former League umpire, Harry Beitzel, organised an unofficial international football competition between the codes, with matches played in New York and Bucharest, the capital of Romania. The first official Australian tour of Ireland took place in 1984, when a team coached by West Australian John Todd (who later coached West Coast Eagles) defeated Ireland 2 Tests to 1. By the 1980s, Ireland was even sending players the other way, with Melbourne ruckman Jim Stynes leading the charge. Stynes won the Brownlow Medal in 1991 and would eventually set the AFL consecutive games record—an unbeaten streak of 244 appearances for the Demons. For Australians, the **INTERNATIONAL RULES** game has two major differences: a round ball and a rectangular field. For the Irish it's contending with tackling, which is not part of Gaelic football. Also, there are three ways to score: a goal (6 points), when the ball is kicked or knocked (not hand-passed) into a soccer-style net; an over (3 points) when the ball goes over the crossbar and between the goalposts; and a behind (1 point), as in Australian football.

### QUICK ? QUIZ

What would be the total number of points if Australia scored 2 goals, 9 overs and 11 behinds in an International Rules series match?
**CLUE:** Don't forget, 6 points for a goal, 3 for an over and 1 for a behind.

### DID YOU KNOW?

Gaelic football players are amateurs—in other words, they are not paid to play their favourite game.

**ADVANCE AUSTRALIA:** Coached by Chris Scott and captained by Hawthorn superstar Shaun Burgoyne, the 2017 Australian International Rules team won by 10 and 3 points in its two Tests against Ireland.

Challenge yourself in order to grow

LAWS OF FOOTY

REAL

SPOT

10

DIFFERENCES

DEGREE OF
DIFFICULTY ★ ★ ☆

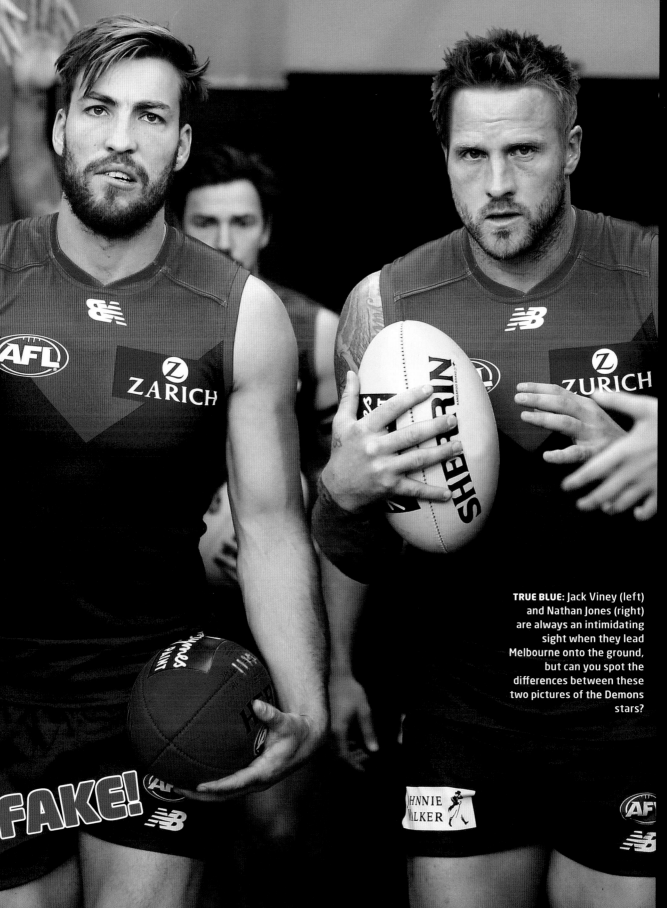

**TRUE BLUE:** Jack Viney (left) and Nathan Jones (right) are always an intimidating sight when they lead Melbourne onto the ground, but can you spot the differences between these two pictures of the Demons stars?

FAKE!

**ESTABLISHED** 1869

**CAPTAIN** Jack Ziebell

**SENIOR COACH** Rhyce Shaw

The North Melbourne Kangaroos are a very old and proud club. They had great success in the 1970s, winning premierships in 1975 and 1977 under super coach Ron Barassi, and then again in 1996 and 1999 under one of the modern-day masters, Denis Pagan. Although they were a battling club in their early days in the League, the Kangaroos have produced a host of champions, none better than Wayne Carey, who was a star throughout the 1990s, and is often rated the best player in the game's long history. The famous Shinboner spirit that seems to get the Roos over the line in many tight matches is alive and well. The Kangas have produced champion players such as Glenn Archer, who, just like current captain **Jack Ziebell (right)**, was as hard as nails. As of 2019, the Roos also have an AFLW team, playing 'home' matches in Melbourne, Hobart and Launceston.

### KANGA'S MAGIC MOMENTS

**1** In the 2014 finals series, the Kangaroos played the Cats in the semi-final. The underdogs pulled off an unbelievable performance to win by 6 points, vaulting them into the Preliminary Final.

**2** Wayne Carey captained the Roos to their 1996 and 1999 premierships. He was a great centre half-forward, and produced one of the greatest individual performances, in round 17, 1996, when he kicked 11 goals against Melbourne at the MCG.

**3** In 2016, club legend **Brent 'Boomer' Harvey (right)** hung up the boots having played a VFL/AFL record 432 senior games. Although his final game didn't go North Melbourne's way, fans had the chance to say goodbye to one of the game's true champions.

## FROM THE BEGINNING

**CLUB FORMED:** 1869

**JOINED THE VFL/AFL:** 1925

**PREMIERSHIPS: 4 -** 1975, 1977, 1996, 1999

**GAMES RECORD-HOLDER:** Brent Harvey (432)

**GOALS RECORD-HOLDER:** Wayne Carey (671)

**JOINED THE AFLW:** 2019

## CLUB SONG

*(TO THE TUNE OF WEE DEOCH AN DORIS)*

So join in the chorus and sing it one and all
Join in the chorus, North Melbourne's on the ball
Good old North Melbourne, we're champions you'll agree
North Melbourne is the team that plays, to win for you and me

Kanga >

## KANGA'S ONE TO WATCH

# 50
# BEN BROWN

Big Ben Brown. Has there ever been a better number 50 in the League? It sure is hard to miss Ben Brown; he stands 200cm tall (not including his hair) and can outmuscle most defenders. He is also one of the most accurate set shots at goal in the AFL, and has perhaps the longest run-up before kicking in the game's history!

# QUICK QUIZ

Three former North Melbourne players have coached other clubs to premierships.

**WHO ARE THEY?**

..........................................

ANSWER

..........................................

..........................................

# DID YOU KNOW?

Between 2007 and 2018, North Melbourne established a record winning streak of 17 straight games against Melbourne. Although this streak came to an end during the 2018 season, it will be hard to top. Interestingly, the club's previous streak was also against Melbourne: 16 from 1976-84.

# NMFC.COM.AU

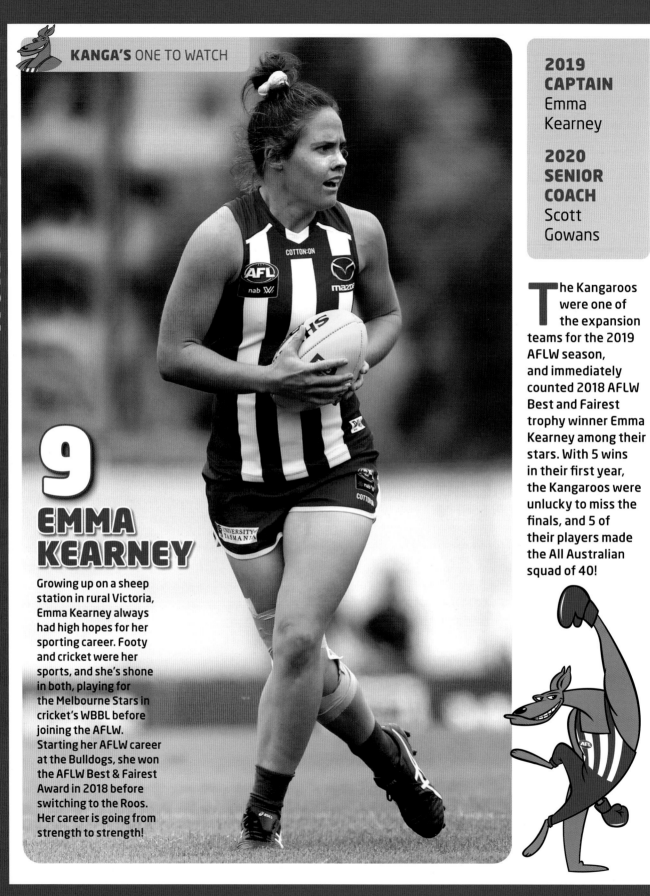

KANGA'S ONE TO WATCH

2019
**CAPTAIN**
Emma
Kearney

2020
**SENIOR COACH**
Scott
Gowans

**9**

# EMMA KEARNEY

Growing up on a sheep station in rural Victoria, Emma Kearney always had high hopes for her sporting career. Footy and cricket were her sports, and she's shone in both, playing for the Melbourne Stars in cricket's WBBL before joining the AFLW. Starting her AFLW career at the Bulldogs, she won the AFLW Best & Fairest Award in 2018 before switching to the Roos. Her career is going from strength to strength!

The Kangaroos were one of the expansion teams for the 2019 AFLW season, and immediately counted 2018 AFLW Best and Fairest trophy winner Emma Kearney among their stars. With 5 wins in their first year, the Kangaroos were unlucky to miss the finals, and 5 of their players made the All Australian squad of 40!

FOOD & FITNESS

# PLAYERS' FITNESS

AFL footballers need to be super fit. The ultimate footballer is a marathon runner, sprinter, high-jumper, wrestler, acrobat and weightlifter—all rolled into one! On-ballers regularly run more than 15 kilometres in a game. The only way to get super fit is to train hard for months—and that's what pre-season training is all about. Most clubs start training in October-November—with the Grand Finalists being the last pair to return to work—and take only a two-week break over the summer holidays as they gear up for the start of the Premiership Season in March. All players undergo fitness testing for speed, stamina and strength, and are expected to maintain or improve on those results. You can work on your fitness by jogging and adding some sprints into the run, having regular kick-to-kick sessions, leading for the ball, like Sydney Swans champion Lance Franklin, and handballing to a friend as you swap ends every now and then. You'll know it's doing you good if you work up a sweat.

**ON YOUR MARK:** Whether you're the fastest or slowest player on the team, you can always work on your running abilities. Burning up the track here are Abbie McKay, Madeline Brancatisano, Natalie Grider and Rebecca Webster during the 2018 AFLW Draft Combine at Marvel Stadium.

## QUICK ? QUIZ

Which Geelong player, whose parents were both top athletes, is regarded by many as the fittest player in the AFL?
**CLUE:** Before embarking on his AFL career, he was a middle-distance runner and steeplechaser who had his sights on a 2012 Olympic appearance.

## DID YOU KNOW?

Big men are now among the most mobile and athletic players in the game. During the 2019 pre-season, Adelaide ruckman Reilly O'Brien (202cm and 101kg) finished third in Adelaide's 2km time trial—well ahead of many more agile teammates.

**ALL ABOUT...** THE GAMES KING

The first player to reach 300 games was Collingwood's great full-forward, Gordon Coventry, in July, 1937. It took another 46 years before the 400-game barrier was broken, in August, 1983, by Richmond's champion rover **Kevin Bartlett.** There are now four players who have played 400 games or more: Essendon full-back **Dustin Fletcher** (400), Bartlett (403), Hawthorn's **Michael Tuck** (426), and the games record-holder, North Melbourne midfielder **Brent Harvey** (432). Harvey played for the Kangaroos for 20 years and nine days, from 1996-2016.

### DID Y⊙U KNOW?

Kevin Sheedy holds the record for the most games—combined—as a player and a coach, with 930! Sheeds played 251 games for Richmond (1967-70), coached Essendon from 1981-2007 (635 games), and GWS GIANTS (2012-13, 44 games). Mick Malthouse is next with 892 games as a player and coach, but he coached more games than any other (718, for Footscray, West Coast, Collingwood and Carlton).

Fletcher has the longest career: 22 years and 58 days, (1993-2015) and is the second oldest player to have played (40 years and 23 days). The oldest is Vic Cumberland (Melbourne and St Kilda), who was 43 years and 50 days when he returned from retirement in 1920, after an absence of 5 years! The youngest on debut was Claude Clough, who was 15 years and 209 days when he played for St Kilda in round 1, 1900. Clough played 22 games for just one win and that was in his first game!

Tuck might be the happiest player to have played the game: he has the most wins (302, and 1 draw), most finals played (39) most Grand Finals (11), and most Premierships (7). What a career! The player who played the most consecutive games is the late Melbourne legend, Jim Stynes, who played 244 games in a row. What an achievement!

**QUICK ❓ QUIZ**

Gordon Coventry was the first player to kick more than 1,000 goals. When he retired, in 1937, he had kicked 1,299 goals.

**WHO NOW HOLDS THE RECORD FOR THE MOST GOALS?**

**CLUE:** He played for St Kilda and Sydney.

**MARATHON MEN:** (from left): Dustin Fletcher (Essendon), Brent Harvey (North Melbourne), Michael Tuck (Hawthorn) and Kevin Bartlett (Richmond) are the four men to reach the 400-game milestone at AFL level. Each was a one-club player and a champion to boot!

## PORT ADELAIDE
### FOOTBALL CLUB

**ESTABLISHED** 1870

**CAPTAIN** Tom Jonas

**SENIOR COACH** Ken Hinkley

**P**ort Adelaide was admitted to the AFL competition in 1997, but the history of the club can be traced to the formation of the SANFL club Port Adelaide in 1870. In 2020 the club celebrates its 150th anniversary. Widely recognised as Australia's most successful football club, the Port Adelaide Magpies collected 36 premierships in the South Australian National Football League, the first in 1884, the most recent in 1999. In 1990, the club applied to join the AFL, but it wasn't until 1994 that a second bid was successful and Port Adelaide was confirmed as the AFL's 16th club. Port Adelaide was the AFL's minor Premier three years straight from 2002 to 2004 and won its first premiership in 2004 under coach Mark Williams, the son of Port Magpies' legend Fos Williams. Port Adelaide has one of the best rivalries in the League against its cross-town enemy, the Adelaide Crows.

### THUNDA'S MAGIC MOMENTS

**1** On Grand Final day 2004, Port Adelaide romped to its first AFL premiership, ending Brisbane's dream of a fourth successive flag. Fans sung long into the night to celebrate the victory.

**2** The Cornes family name is royalty in Adelaide, with Graham Cornes inducted into the Australian Football Hall of Fame in 2012. He was also the first coach of the Crows in 1991. Ironically his sons, Chad and Kane, were Port heroes. In round 8, 2015, Kane played his 300th game for the Power, and promptly retired. He remains the club's games record holder.

**3** The first Port Adelaide-Adelaide Crows Showdown in 2018 was a game for the ages. In a see-sawing contest, in the final play of the game, down by less than a goal, Steve Motlop burst towards goal and slammed it home to win the game for the Power!

## FROM THE BEGINNING

**CLUB FORMED:** 1870
**JOINED THE AFL:** 1997
**PREMIERSHIPS: 1** - 2004
**GAMES RECORD-HOLDER:** Kane Cornes (300)
**GOALS RECORD-HOLDER:** Warren Tredrea (549)

## CLUB SONG

**(WRITTEN FOR THE CLUB BY QUENTIN EYERS AND LES KACZMAREK)**

We've got the Power to win
Power to rule
Come on, Port Adelaide aggression
We are the Power from Port
It's more than a sport
It's the true Port Adelaide tradition
We'll never stop, stop, stop
'Til we're top, top, top
There's history here in the making
We've got the Power to win
We'll never give in
'Til the flag is ours for the taking
POWER!

Thunda Power >

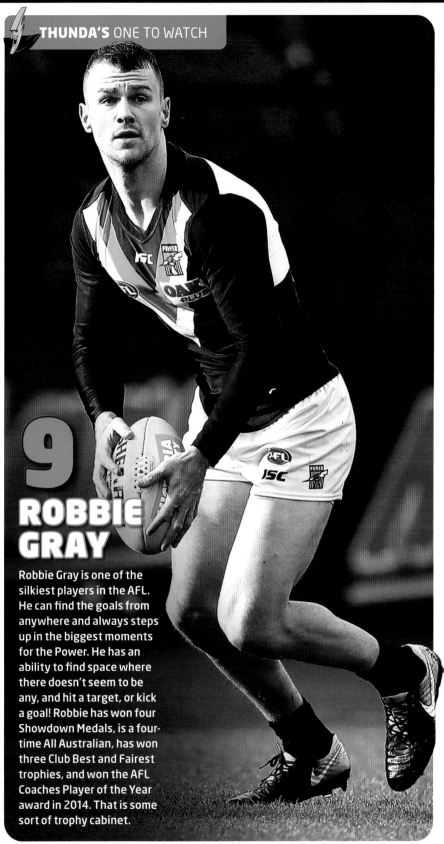

# 9
# ROBBIE GRAY

Robbie Gray is one of the silkiest players in the AFL. He can find the goals from anywhere and always steps up in the biggest moments for the Power. He has an ability to find space where there doesn't seem to be any, and hit a target, or kick a goal! Robbie has won four Showdown Medals, is a four-time All Australian, has won three Club Best and Fairest trophies, and won the AFL Coaches Player of the Year award in 2014. That is some sort of trophy cabinet.

## QUICK QUIZ

Two Port Adelaide players have kicked 8 goals in a match. The first was in 1998 and the second in 2014.

**WHO WERE THE PLAYERS?**

**CLUE:** One was the acting captain in the 2004 Grand Final and the other joined the Power in 2010 from Richmond.

.............................................
ANSWER
.............................................

## DID YOU KNOW?

Port Adelaide hardmen Byron Pickett and Damien Hardwick joined an elite band of AFL players after the Power's victory in the 2004 Grand Final. They became the 22nd and 23rd players to be selected in Premiership teams at two clubs. Pickett was a premiership player with the Kangaroos in 1999 and Hardwick celebrated a Grand Final victory with the Bombers in 2000.

# PORTADELAIDE FC.COM.AU

# ON REFLECTION

## When is a free kick not a free kick?

Hold a mirror at right angles to this page just above the word FREE and see what happens. You'll notice that the word FREE is reversed, but what happens to the word KICK?

Before the goal umpire can signal a score—whether goal or behind—what instruction must come from the field umpire?

FREE KICK

## DID Y♥U KNOW?

An umpire can award a free kick against a player or official who deliberately shakes a goal or behind post while a player is lining up or kicking for goal.

**TAKING CHARGE:** Eleni Glouftsis became the first female AFL field umpire in 2017.

# DRIPPING WET

A footy property steward was on the way to the Adelaide Oval for an AFL Auskick clinic when he fell into the River Torrens. On his way out of the water, he dropped some essential gear. Help him find these five items.

**DEGREE OF DIFFICULTY** ★ ☆ ☆

Maintain the work rate

### DID YOU KNOW?
It took 2½ years to build Marvel Stadium —and about 80,000 cubic metres of concrete. That's enough to fill 400 Olympic-sized swimming pools!

REAL

**DEGREE OF DIFFICULTY** ★ ★ ☆

# SPOT
# 10
# DIFFERENCES

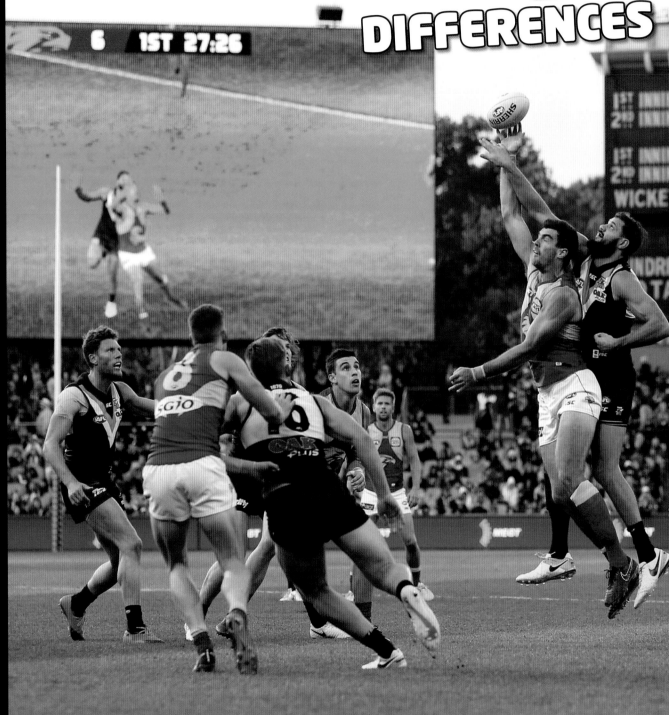

**FAKE!**

**RICH HISTORY:** Now that footy is back at the Adelaide Oval, it's not just cricket fans who can enjoy the look of the ground's famous old scoreboard.

**SPEAKING OF LOOKING, CAN YOU SPOT THE TEN DIFFERENCES IN THESE IMAGES?**

**RICHMOND**
EST 1885

**ESTABLISHED** 1885

**CAPTAIN** Trent Cotchin

**SENIOR COACH** Damien Hardwick

When it comes to supporters, you won't find any more passionate—or one-eyed—than Richmond fans. It's a tradition that stretches back to the club's first game in 1885, although the famous yellow and black did not join the League until 1908. Back then, the Tigers were known as the Yellow and Black Angels or the Wasps, until a Richmond fan coined the phrase 'Eat 'em alive, Tigers' in the 1920s. The club won consecutive flags in 1920-21, but its golden era was between 1967 and 1980 when the Tigers won five premierships, four of them when coached by club immortal Tom Hafey. The Tigers struggled after their 1980 triumph, but returned to the top in the 2017 finals, culminating in a thrashing of Adelaide in the Grand Final. The Tigers will have a team in the AFLW from 2020.

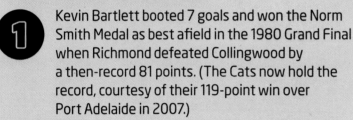

**TIGER'S** MAGIC MOMENTS

**1** Kevin Bartlett booted 7 goals and won the Norm Smith Medal as best afield in the 1980 Grand Final when Richmond defeated Collingwood by a then-record 81 points. (The Cats now hold the record, courtesy of their 119-point win over Port Adelaide in 2007.)

**2** The 2017 Grand Final. What a game. The Tiger Army was up and roaring and nothing was going to stop them. After trailing by 9 points at quarter-time, the Tigers kicked 14 goals to Adelaide's 4 to a break a 37-year Premiership drought.

**3** Jack Higgins decided to miss his last year of school in 2017, to concentrate on footy. He made his debut for the Tigers in 2018, and instantly became a fan favourite. His season highlight was winning the AFL's goal of the year, with a remarkable 'around the post' goal against Collingwood in round 19.

Tiger 'Stripes' Dyer >

## FROM THE BEGINNING

**CLUB FORMED:** 1885
**JOINED THE VFL/AFL:** 1908
**PREMIERSHIPS:** 12 - 1920-21, 1932, 1934, 1943, 1967, 1969, 1973-74, 1980, 2017, 2019
**GAMES RECORD-HOLDER:** Kevin Bartlett (403)
**GOALS RECORD-HOLDER:** Jack Titus (970)
**JOINING THE AFLW:** 2020

## CLUB SONG

(TO THE TUNE OF ROW, ROW, ROW)

Oh, we're from Tigerland
A fighting fury we're from Tigerland
In any weather you will see us with a grin
Risking head and shin
If we're behind then never mind
We'll fight and fight and win
For we're from Tigerland
We never weaken 'til the final siren's gone
Like the Tiger of old
We're strong and we're bold
For we're from Tiger
– YELLOW AND BLACK
We're from Tigerland

**SASH'S** ONE TO WATCH

# 4
# DUSTIN MARTIN

Dustin Martin is a one-man wrecking ball. He has one of the most damaging 'don't argues' in the game, making him almost impossible to tackle. 'Dusty' is a dominant midfielder, but when he goes forward, LOOK OUT! In 2017, he had one of the greatest years of all time, taking out the Brownlow Medal, AFLPA MVP award, the Norm Smith Medal and a Premiership Medal. No other player in the game's history has won that quartet in one season. He showed his brilliance again in the 2019 Finals Series, booting six goals in Richmond's qualifying win over the Brisbane Lions, and then won his second Norm Smith Medal, after a four-goal spree in the Grand Final.

# QUICK QUIZ

Richmond coach Damien Hardwick was, as his name suggests, a very hard player. He became a multiple premiership player with two clubs.

**WHO WERE THEY?**

**CLUE:** One has a red sash and the other a white and teal V.

**ANSWER**

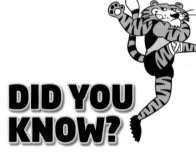

# DID YOU KNOW?

In 1972, Richmond's 22.18 (150) equalled the previous highest score kicked in a Grand Final, by Essendon in the 1946 decider. The problem for the Tigers was that Carlton won the match with a record tally of 28.9 (177). Richmond's 150 points is the highest-ever losing total in the decider and the aggregate match score of 327 points is also a League record.

# RICHMONDFC. COM.AU

RICHMOND

CLUB ZONE

# WHAT'S IN A NAME?

So you reckon you're up to speed with all the AFL clubs and their nicknames? So do you know where the Mayblooms fit in? Or the Fuchsias? Believe it or not, the fearsome Hawks were once known as the Mayblooms, named after a tree, the hawthorn, which flowered during the footy season. Melbourne has a similar story to tell. The Demons—a great name—were onced named after a flower, the fuchsia. How scary is that? Going the other way, the Swans, graceful and elegant birds, were once the Blood-Stained Angels and the Bloods. Fitzroy, which merged with Brisbane in 1996, were the Gorillas before they became the Lions; the Kangaroos were the Shinboners (relating to the abattoirs near Arden Street, according to some); the Tigers were the Wasps; the Bulldogs the Tricolours, and the Bombers the Same Old, as in 'the same old' team wins the flag again!

## QUICK ? QUIZ

The Swans' 1955 Brownlow Medallist Fred Goldsmith is the only player in this position to win the Medal.

**WHICH POSITION?**

**CLUE:** It's not full-forward, although only one full-forward, Tony Lockett (1987) has won the Medal.

## DID Y⚽U KNOW?

Former Geelong champion **Garry 'Buddha' Hocking (right)** changed his name to 'Whiskas' for one match, round 12, 1999, to raise funds for the Cats through a sponsorship deal. That name even appeared in the Football Record.

SOUTH MELBOURNE

COME ON THE BLOODS

## ALL ABOUT... WINNERS & LOSERS

**W**e all love to go home a **WINNER** after a match, but of course that doesn't always happen. There have been some huge margins—the biggest ever was in 1979 when Fitzroy thumped Melbourne by 190 points—and, of course, many one-point thrillers and draws. The Grand Finals in 1948, 1977 and 2010 ended in draws and had to be replayed. One match even took four days to decide. The lights went out in the round 10 match between Essendon and St Kilda at Waverley Park in 1996 and had to be concluded the following Tuesday evening. Nobody could ever forget the round 6 clash in 1989 when the Hawks played Geelong. Hawthorn was 56 points behind at the 28-minute mark of the second quarter, but fought back to win by 8 points. It was the third highest-scoring game in history, the Hawks winning 26.15.171 to Geelong's 25.13.163. The match with the most goals was between St Kilda (31 goals) and Melbourne (21), in round 6, 1978 at the MCG.

**QUICK ? QUIZ**

Carlton won 20 home and away games on its way to the 1995 AFL premiership, losing only twice.

**WHICH TEAMS MANAGED TO BEAT THEM THAT YEAR?**

**CLUE:** Premiership defender Sean Dempster played for each of these teams.

**ALL TIED UP:** There is no scoreboard more thrilling than one with scores locked level at full-time, and that's what happened in the 1977 Grand Final between North Melbourne and Collingwood. When they came back a week later, the Roos won the re-match!

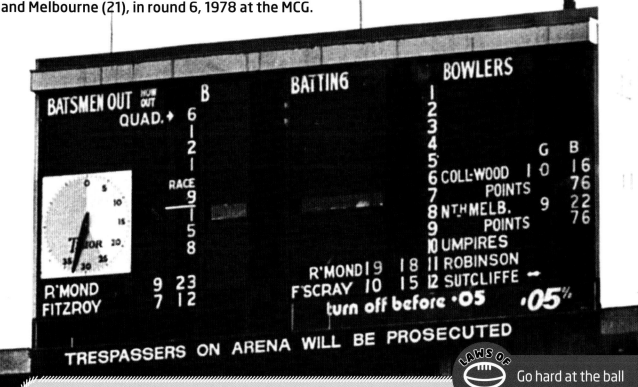

**LAWS OF FOOTY**
Go hard at the ball

**DID YOU KNOW?**
Geelong holds the record for the highest score in an AFL match. The Cats booted 37.17 (239) to Brisbane's 11.9 (75) at Carrara in round 7, 1992.

**JUMPING JACK:** With three Coleman Medals, two best and fairest awards and two Tigers Premierships (2017, 2019), Richmond ace Jack Riewoldt is a star. He confirmed his status as one of the game's great forwards with five goals in Richmond's 2019 Grand Final victory.

# COLOUR ME IN!

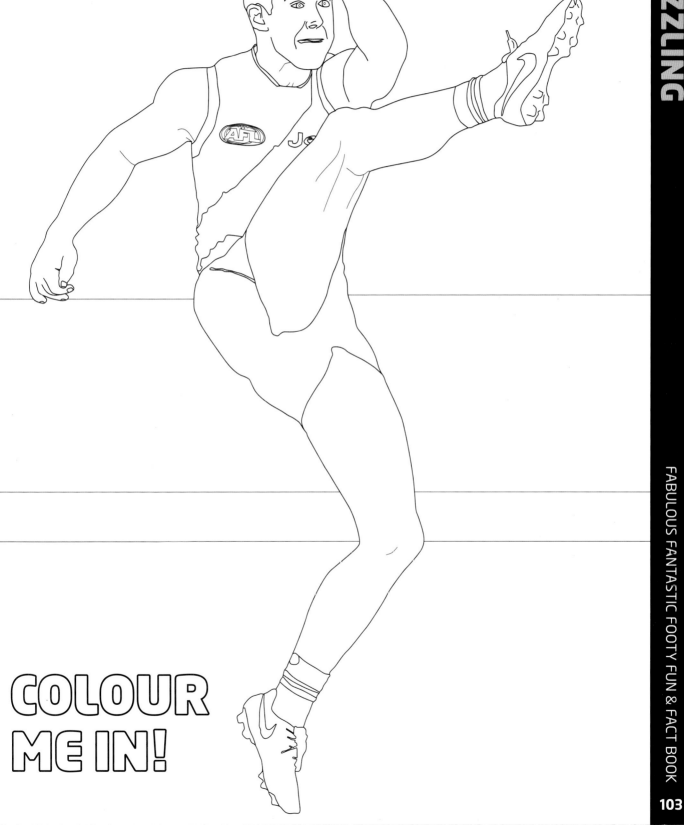

COLOUR
ME IN!

**ESTABLISHED** 1873

**CAPTAIN** Jarryn Geary

**SENIOR COACH** Brett Ratten

U nlikely victories, near misses, plenty of cheers and tears—there's never been a dull moment for the St Kilda Football Club. Supporting the Saints has always been a rollercoaster ride for their loyal legion of fans. Were you watching in 1997 when the Saints lost the Grand Final against Adelaide after leading at half-time? How about the drawn Grand Final in 2010? That moment near the end when the ball bounced out of Stephen Milne's grasp? The Saints have had four home grounds, played in seven Grand Finals and won one historic flag, way back in 1966, and that by a solitary point. Some of the best players to kick a footy have worn the famous red, white and black, including Robert Harvey and Ian Stewart (two and three Brownlow Medals respectively) and legendary goalkickers Tony Lockett and **Nick Riewoldt (left).** Despite the club's lack of success, the Saints have had eight Brownlow winners. St Kilda will join Gold Coast, Richmond and West Coast in entering the AFLW competition for the 2020 season.

## FROM THE BEGINNING

CLUB FORMED: **1873**
JOINED THE VFL/AFL: **1897**
PREMIERSHIPS: **1 - 1966**
GAMES RECORD-HOLDER:
Robert Harvey (383)
GOALS RECORD-HOLDER:
Tony Lockett (898)
JOINING THE AFLW: **2020**

## CLUB SONG

(TO THE TUNE OF *WHEN THE SAINTS GO MARCHING IN*)

Oh when the Saints
go marching in
Oh when the Saints
go marching in
Oh how I want to
be with St Kilda
When the Saints go
marching in

### TREVOR'S MAGIC MOMENTS

**1** That wobbly point! With scores level in the 1966 Grand Final against Collingwood, and with just minutes to go, Barry Breen kicked a behind to give the Saints their first— and only—Premiership.

**2** Back-to-back Brownlows. Running machine **Robert Harvey (right)** won the Brownlow Medal in 1997 and 1998—but Saints fans already knew he was a champion.

**3** In 2009 the Saints won the first 19 games of the season, their best winning sequence in club history, giving them the minor Premiership.

Trevor 'Saint' Kilda >

TREVOR'S ONE TO WATCH

## 4
## JADE GRESHAM

Rising star Jade Gresham had a breakout season in 2018 and looks ready to take the League by storm. He is superb around the goals, with so many tricks and skills that fans are wondering what he will do next.

# QUICK QUIZ

## HOW MANY TIMES HAVE THE SAINTS FINISHED ON THE BOTTOM OF THE LADDER?

**CLUE:** Saints hero Barry Breen, who kicked the behind that sealed St Kilda's 1966 Premiership victory had this guernsey number on that famous day.

......................................

ANSWER

# DID YOU KNOW?

No team has waited longer than St Kilda for its first Flag. The Saints, one of the League's foundation clubs in 1897, finally came marching in and won that long-awaited Premiership in 1966, a gap of 70 seasons.

SWITCHEROO: Until the 1990s, players had a tradition of swapping jumpers with their opponents at the end of Grand Finals. So, when the Saints won their only flag in 1966, their captain Darrel 'Doc' Baldock was wearing a Pies guernsey, and Collingwood skipper Des Tuddenham was in Doc's Saints one!

# SAINTS.COM.AU

**ALL ABOUT...** FOOTY BOOTS

The earliest **FOOTBALL BOOTS** weren't really football boots at all, when compared to the slick footwear players wear today. Quite often players would just hammer leather stops into the bottom of their ankle-high work boots. Before games the umpire would run his hand along the soles to make sure no nails were sticking out! Until the mid 1970s, all players wore black boots, usually off the shelf, but soon coloured boots—white was first—joined in. These days anything goes: green, pink, orange, silver, blue, yellow, and sometimes all mixed and matched. In the annual Indigenous round, some Indigenous players will have their boots specially made with colours and images important to their culture. All senior players will have their boots made to suit, and they will have several pairs, with long stops for wet days. Lucky, aren't they?

**QUICK ? QUIZ**

A Brownlow Medallist of the 1980s was nicknamed SUPERBOOT, because of his long and straight kicking.

**CAN YOU NAME HIM?**

**CLUE:** He started his career at Footscray and won the Brownlow Medal with Fitzroy, sharing it with another player who switched from Footscray to South Melbourne.

**DID YOU KNOW?**

One of the first players to wear coloured boots was the TV star John 'Sammy' Newman, who shocked traditionalists with a set of white boots in the early 1970s.

28 of 132 — JOHN NEWMAN — RUCK GEELONG — HAVE FUN WITH SCANLENS GUM

## ALL ABOUT... ONE GAME FOR ALL

**P**eople of all races and nationalities play Australian Football. Names such as Jesaulenko, Silvagni, Daicos, Koutoufides and Rocca are among the most recognised in the game, as are those of Aboriginal stars such as Long, Krakouer, Winmar and Rioli. Football is a great leveller; people from all walks of life are equal on the footy field. Thankfully, due to the AFL's Racial and Religious Vilification policy, today's players with multicultural backgrounds don't have to endure insults, and are made to feel welcome and valued for their brilliant contributions to the AFL. It's a game for all to enjoy.

**UNITED:** The AFL embraces multiculturalism as this 2017 photo, at the launch of the multicultural ambassadors from across clubs clearly demonstrates:

**BACK ROW (L-R):** Adam Saad, Lin Jong, Dyson Heppell, Jason Johannisen, Akec Makur Chuot , Jake Kolodjashnij. **MIDDLE ROW (L-R):** Stephen Coniglio, Tom Nicholls  Jimmy Toumpas, Majak Daw, Helen Rodan, Christian Salem, Bachar Houli. **CROUCHING (L-R):** Allir Aliir, Darcy Vescio, David Zaharakis.

**DID YOU KNOW?**
Former Fremantle captain Peter Bell was born in Korea and adopted by a couple from Western Australia.

**QUICK QUIZ**
Former Brisbane Lions full-back Mal Michael was born in a country just north of Queensland. **WHAT IS THE NAME OF THAT COUNTRY? CLUE:** Hawthorn regularly takes its player there for a team-building trek along the Kokoda Trail.

FOOD & FITNESS

# SELECTION TIPS

**D**oes grocery shopping with your mum or dad bore you to tears? We've got a challenge for you: become their expert fruit and vegetable (F&V) selector.

If you want to be healthy, experts say you should eat three to five servings of vegetables and two to four servings of fruit every day. Obviously it's important that the F&V are fresh and taste good, so the selection process is more important than picking the best line-up for the weekend's match! Experts also say variety is important and that you should eat as many colours as possible—dark-green leafy vegetables, as well as yellow, orange and red fruits and vegetables. That makes sense; you wouldn't want a team full of tall forwards. Here are our tips.

## AVOCADOS

Look for avocados that have a dark green skin without spots. To test if an avocado is ripe, hold it in your hand and (very!) gently press the top of the avocado around the stalk end. If the flesh gives just a little, the avocado is ripe; if your finger easily leaves a dent, it may not be much use for anything except mashing up into an avocado dip. And here's another tip: if you want to ripen an avocado fast, stick it in the fruit bowl with some bananas. (By the way, avocado lovers swear by the Hass variety. Look out for it.)

## BANANAS

Colour is important. Ripe bananas are yellow and spot-free; the only green should be on the tips and brown spotty ones are either old or they've been refrigerated. Either way, they'll only be good for smoothies or muffins. Buy green ones if you're not in a hurry to eat them and they'll ripen in the fruit bowl. Look out for the smaller Lady Finger bananas—they're sweeter than the big Cavendish variety and great for snacks.

## DID YU KNOW?

The apple is a member of the rose family and there are more than 7,000 varieties grown throughout the world—some the size of a cherry and others bigger than a grapefruit. An apple expert is called a pomologist.

## CARROTS

Next time you're shopping, take a close look at the carrots. Some are long and skinny with tapering tips; others are shorter and fatter and have rounded tips. The short, fat ones are likely to be much sweeter than the skinny ones. And make sure your carrots are as hard as nails; if they bend without snapping, they're not very fresh.

## MANGOES

Great mangoes should have that wonderful mango smell, so sniff the fruit to check. A ripe mango will give just a little when you press it (gently!) and have a lovely deep orange colour. (Like avocados, unripe mangoes will ripen quickly if you leave them with bananas in a bowl.) Steer clear of mangoes that have dark spots.

## POTATOES

As with bananas, green is BAD. It means they've been exposed to the sun while growing (remember, they do grow under the ground) and could taste bitter. Look for potatoes that are firm and without sprouts. Different varieties are good for different things: the common Sebago is good for boiling, mashing and baking, while Pink Fir and Pontiacs are better not mashed.

## WATERMELON

Tap, tap, tap: good watermelons shouldn't sound hollow when you tap them. They should be nice and heavy for their size (like oranges). Look out for the seedless varieties—though there go those backyard, seed-spitting competitions!

## ORANGES

Good oranges should be so heavy that you almost need to be a weightlifter to lift them. That will mean they're holding a lot of juice. And don't be fooled by slightly green oranges—they can be juicier than the deeply coloured orange ones.

## ZUCCHINI

Those really big ones might make a great photograph, but they're not going to have much flavour. Look for small firm ones that are dark, shiny and unscarred. The large ones will do for stuffing, but aren't great for other things. Did you know that in France, zucchini are called courgettes and, in America, they're called squash?

LAWS OF FOOTY — Win as a team

## SYDNEY SWANS

**ESTABLISHED** 1874
Moved to Sydney in 1982

**2019 CAPTAINS** Josh Kennedy,
Luke Parker & Dane Rampe

**SENIOR COACH** John Longmire

The Sydney Swans have only been swanning around the Harbour City since 1982, when the team flew from its base at the Lake Oval in South Melbourne. Originally the South Melbourne Footy Club, the club changed its nickname in the 1930s when a football writer suggested there were so many West Australian players in the team that it should be known as the Swans. (Western Australia's bird emblem is the black swan). At that time the club was also known as 'the Blood-Stained Angels' or 'the Bloods', because of their white and red uniform. The nickname brought the club some luck as it won the 1933 flag to add to its 1909 and 1918 triumphs, but it wasn't until 2005 that they broke back through to win their next Premiership. The Swans are one of the most successful teams in the AFL era, and also won the flag in 2012.

### SYD'S MAGIC MOMENTS

**1** Tony Lockett kicked the winning behind after the final siren to defeat Essendon by one point in the 1996 Preliminary Final at the SCG. It put the Swans into their first Grand Final in 51 years, but, sadly, the red and white went down to the Kangaroos, despite Lockett kicking 6 goals.

**2** Deep into the last quarter of the 2005 Grand Final, up by less than a goal, West Coast made a last gasp effort send the ball inside 50, only for Swans hero Leo Barry to fly across the pack and take the mark, sealing the win! Stephen Quartermain on Network Ten's broadcast made the immortal cry, 'LEO BARRY YOU STAR!'

**3** When presented with the Premiership Cup in 2005, coach Paul Roos raised it high, and yelled: 'Here it is!' It was the first Premiership for the Swans since 1933, and the first time the club had received a Cup on Grand Final day. The Premier team first received a Cup in 1959.

Syd 'Swannie' Skilton >

## FROM THE BEGINNING

**CLUB FORMED:** 1874
**JOINED THE VFL/AFL:** 1897
**MOVED TO SYDNEY:** 1982
**PREMIERSHIPS: 5 -** 1909, 1918, 1933, 2005, 2012
**GAMES RECORD-HOLDER:** Adam Goodes (372)
**GOALS RECORD-HOLDER:** Bob Pratt (681)

## CLUB SONG

(TO THE TUNE OF THE NOTRE DAME VICTORY MARCH)

Cheer, cheer the red and the white
Honour the name by day and by night
Lift that noble banner high
Shake down the thunder from the sky
Whether the odds be great or small
Swans will go in and win overall
While her loyal sons are marching
Onwards to victory

## SYD'S ONE TO WATCH

# 23
# LANCE FRANKLIN

Lance 'Buddy' Franklin is one of the greatest forwards in the game's history. His versatility for a big man is remarkable, and his pin-point kicking among the best ever. In 2018, he became the ninth player to pass the 900-goal mark. He has been an All Australian eight times, won one best and fairest (at Hawthorn), as well as winning the Coleman Medal four times. In 2018, he was named captain of the All Australian team, although he has never captained at club level.

# QUICK QUIZ

Sydney's best and fairest trophy is named after the greatest player to play for South Melbourne?

**CAN YOU NAME HIM?**

**CLUE:** He won three Brownlow Medals.

............................................
**ANSWER**
............................................

# DID YOU KNOW?

Swans players have won more Brownlow Medals than any other club. **Bob Skilton** heads the list with three (1959, 1963 and 1968)—what a bobby dazzler! The others are Herbie Matthews (1940), Ron Clegg (1949), Fred Goldsmith (1955), Peter Bedford (1970), Graham Teasdale (1977), Barry Round (1981), Greg Williams (1986), Gerard Healy (1988), Paul Kelly (1995) and Adam Goodes (2003, 2006). That makes 14 Brownlows!

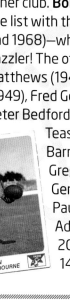

3 BOB SKILTON
SOUTH MELBOURNE

# SYDNEYSWANS. COM.AU

FABULOUS FANTASTIC FOOTY FUN & FACT BOOK

Tony Lockett's best season tally of goals came in 1992 when he kicked 132 goals in 22 games.

**WHAT WAS HIS AVERAGE PER GAME IN 1992?**

Tony Lockett played 281 games of AFL footy for two clubs (St Kilda 183 games, Sydney 98) between 1983 and 2002. He kicked 1,360 goals, breaking the record set by Collingwood full-forward Gordon Coventry (1,299 goals, 306 games, 1920-37). Lockett, nicknamed 'Plugger', a nickname he shared with his father, Howard, was huge in every way; big, strong, powerful and very fast for his size. Added to that was a bag of skills that every forward should have: strong hands like a vice, great sense of when and where to lead, and a long and accurate kick.

He is one of only five players to have kicked more than 1,000 goals—the others are Coventry, Jason Dunstall (Hawthorn, 1985-98, 1,254 goals), Doug Wade (Geelong, North Melbourne, 1961-75, 1,057) and Gary Ablett senior (Hawthorn and Geelong, 1,031 goals, 1982, 1984-96).

Lockett averaged 4.84 goals per game, but that's not the record: that is held by Hawthorn's Peter Hudson (1967-74, 1977), who kicked 727 goals in only 129 games for an average of 5.64. Hudson's average was just ahead of Essendon's John Coleman (1949-54, 98 games, 537 goals, average 5.48). Lockett, Coventry, Hudson and Coleman are all Legends of the Australian Football Hall of Fame.

## DID YOU KNOW?

The record for the highest number of goals in one match is held by Melbourne's **Fred Fanning (right)** who kicked 18 goals and 1 behind against St Kilda in the final round of the 1947 season. He didn't play another League game, finishing his career for Hamilton and Coleraine in Victoria's western district. Jason Dunstall's best was 17.5 (against Richmond in 1992), and Tony Lockett's was 16.0 against Fitzroy in 1995.

**GOALS RECORD-HOLDER:** Tony Lockett prepares to kick.

LAWS OF FOOTY

Support your teammates

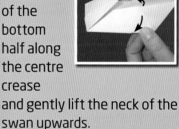

# ORIGAMI SWAN

**O**rigami is the ancient Japanese art of creating birds, animals, flowers and other shapes from paper. 'Ori' means folding, and 'gami' comes from 'kami', meaning paper. Follow these instructions to make a swan—even if you don't barrack for them!

**DEGREE OF DIFFICULTY**  ★ ★ ☆

**1** Start with a square piece of paper—any paper will do—and place it in front of you on an angle so it is in a diamond shape.

**2** Fold the square in half to form a centre crease, then unfold

**3** Fold the left and right corners to the centre to make a kite shape.

**4** Turn the paper over and repeat.

**5** Fold the kite shape across the middle so that the lower tip sits near the top tip.

**6** Fold the upper tip back down. This is the swan's head.

**7** Fold down the sides of the bottom half along the centre crease and gently lift the neck of the swan upwards.

**8** Pinch the base of the swan's head so it is looking forward.

## CONGRATULATIONS, YOU'VE DONE IT!

## QUICK ? QUIZ

The Swans hold some impressive records: most Brownlow Medals at one club, and also one of their champions has the record for the most goals in a season—150, in 1934, shared with Hawthorn's Peter Hudson.

### WHO WAS HE?

**CLUE** He was one of the 12 Legends named in 1996, when the Australian Football Hall of Fame was born.

### DID YOU KNOW?

Even when times were tough for the Swans, Sydney fans had plenty of brilliant players to cheer on—the club has produced 11 Brownlow Medallists! The most recent were **Adam Goodes (right)** (2003 and 2006), Paul Kelly (1995), Gerard Healy (1988) and Greg 'Diesel' Williams (1986).

QUICK ❓ QUIZ
The MCG has the largest capacity (100,024). Which current AFL venue has the second largest capacity? **CLUE:** It's also the newest stadium.

## ALL ABOUT... GREAT CROWDS

**W**hen it comes to **BIG CROWDS**, you can't go past the MCG. The 'home' of AFL footy holds a record that may stand forever. An Amazing 121,696 people watched the 1970 Grand Final between Collingwood and Carlton, and the ground also has the record for the most at a home and away game, 99,256, round 10, 1958, between Melbourne and Collingwood. Back in the 1950s, supporters even sat inside the boundary line on Grand Final day! Waverley Park in Melbourne used to draw big crowds. In round 11, 1981, Hawthorn defeated Collingwood there in front of a ground record of 92,935 people. Outside Victoria, Sydney's Stadium Australia (the Olympic Stadium) holds the record for biggest AFL crowd. In 2003, 72,393 people watched Collingwood upset the Swans.

**BEAUTY:** Alex Jesaulenko of the Blues contests for the ball in the pack during the 1970 AFL Grand Final between Carlton and Collingwood at the MCG.

**DID Y⊙U KNOW?**
Footy crowds are one thing, but when the MCG hosted American evangelist Billy Graham in 1959, Melburnians filled every available space. Estimates of the crowd that day range from 130,000 to 143,750!

Provide a strong presence for the team

LAWS OF FOOTY

114

No game of football would be possible without the men and women in white (or red or orange or blue). Until 1975, just one field **UMPIRE** took charge of the game, but since 1993, three field umpires have been making the decisions. The Acme Thunderer has been the whistle of choice for more than a century, after first being used by umpire John Trait in a match between Fitzroy and Carlton in 1886 (nine years before the first AFL/VFL game). In 2019 Shane McInerney passed 500 games umpired, before retiring at the end of the season with 502 games umpired, a League record. Do you know what was special about the Lions v Richmond match in round 6, 1998? That was when goal umpire **KATRINA PRESSLEY (right)** became the first female to officiate in an AFL game. If you'd like to make your own goal umpires' flag, you'll need two pieces of white material 42 centimetres by 54 centimetres and a stick about 75 centimetres long. And don't forget to wait for the field umpire to signal 'all clear' before waving the flags!

**AUTHORITY:** They might not get the same attention as players, but the match-day officials—field, boundary and goal umpires—are a vital component of every AFL game. Umpiring is fun and rewarding, and the ultimate accolade is being selected on the League's day of days: the Grand Final! From left: Steve Piperno, Mark Thomson, Chris Gordon, Shaun Ryan, Brett Rosebury, Matt Stevic, Nathan Marantelli, Nathan Doig, Steve Williams.

## WEST COAST EAGLES

**ESTABLISHED** 1986

**CAPTAIN** Luke Shuey

**SENIOR COACH** Adam Simpson

The Eagles were an unknown quantity when they joined the AFL in 1987, but it didn't take long to find out they meant business. West Coast won 11 games in their first season, including both matches against the Hawks, who were the reigning Premiers! Within five years the club was celebrating a Premiership of its own, beating Geelong in the 1992 decider. Two years later, in 1994, the west was the best again as the Eagles snared their second flag, again over Geelong. So often contenders when September arrives, they have won a further two Premierships, in 2006 and 2018—both by less than a goal! Since the AFL competition was founded in 1990, only Hawthorn (5) has won more flags than the Eagles (4). In the 2020 season, the Eagles will become the second team from WA to be a part of the AFLW.

### RICK'S MAGIC MOMENTS

**1** The Eagles made history in 1992 by beating Geelong and becoming the first non-Victorian winners of the AFL Premiership. It was sweet relief after they'd experienced a disappointing loss to Hawthorn in the 1991 decider—the only Grand Final to be played at Waverley Park.

**2** The Eagles got revenge for their narrow loss in the 2005 Grand Final, beating Sydney by one point in the 2006 Grand Final. Their coach that day was John Worsfold, West Coast's captain for the '92 and '94 Flags!

**3** Late in the last quarter of the 2018 Grand Final, with the Eagles trailing by a point, **Dom Sheed (left)** marked deep in the forward pocket, and, from a difficult angle, slotted the match-winning goal against the Magpies.

Rick 'The Rock' Eagle >

## FROM THE BEGINNING

CLUB FORMED: 1986
JOINED THE AFL: 1987
PREMIERSHIPS: 4 - 1992, 1994, 2006, 2018
GAMES RECORD-HOLDER: Dean Cox (290)
GOALS RECORD-HOLDER: Josh Kennedy (600)
JOINING THE AFLW: 2020

## CLUB SONG

(SONG COMPOSED BY KEVIN PEEK)

We're the Eagles
the West Coast Eagles
And we're here to
show you why
We're the big birds
kings of the big game
We're the Eagles
we're flying high
We're flying high
we're flying high
We're flying high

**RICK'S** ONE TO WATCH

# 17
# JOSH KENNEDY

Josh Kennedy is a two-time Coleman medallist, three-time All Australian, and is West Coast's all-time leading goalkicker. After playing 22 games in two seasons for Carlton, Kennedy was traded out west—as part of the deal that saw 2006 West Coast captain Chris Judd move to the Blues—and has made it his home, becoming one of the best forwards in the game.

# QUICK QUIZ

In West Coast's 2018 AFL Grand Final victory, **Lewis Jetta (below)** won his second Premiership medal.

**WITH WHICH CLUB DID HE WIN HIS FIRST AFL FLAG?**

**CLUE:** Their mascot is also a bird.

ANSWER

# DID YOU KNOW?

West Coast's home ground, Perth Stadium (Optus Stadium) is the newest AFL ground in the country, and is now Perth's number one facility for both football and cricket; it has the second largest capacity in the AFL, behind the MCG. The first AFL game there was staged in round 1, 2018, and was played between West Coast and their long-time rival, Sydney. The Swans spoiled the party, but Eagles fans would have the last laugh in 2018!

# WESTCOAST EAGLES.COM.AU

E very player and every team starts every season with one aim: to win the Premiership. To do that, you don't necessarily have to be the best team through the season, but you DO have to be the best team through the finals. Your first aim is to make the final eight, but since the final eight was introduced in 1994, only Adelaide (1998, 5th) and the Western Bulldogs (2016, 7th) have won the Premiership from outside the top four. No wonder all coaches aim to be in that quartet to give themselves the quickest route to the Grand Final. Teams from fifth to eighth have to win three times to get to the Grand Final, while those in the top four only have to win twice. Premiership players receive a Premiership Medal, and, since 2001, the Premiership coach has received the Jock McHale Medal; the club receives a famous Cup—presented on Grand Final day since 1959—and a Flag, which is presented to the club president at the next season's launch, and is then unfurled at the club's first home game the following season. The wooden spoon is not really an award, but it is the slang 'award' for the team that finished last on the table. This is one 'award' no team wishes to 'win', but it does give that team the first pick in the next year's National Draft.

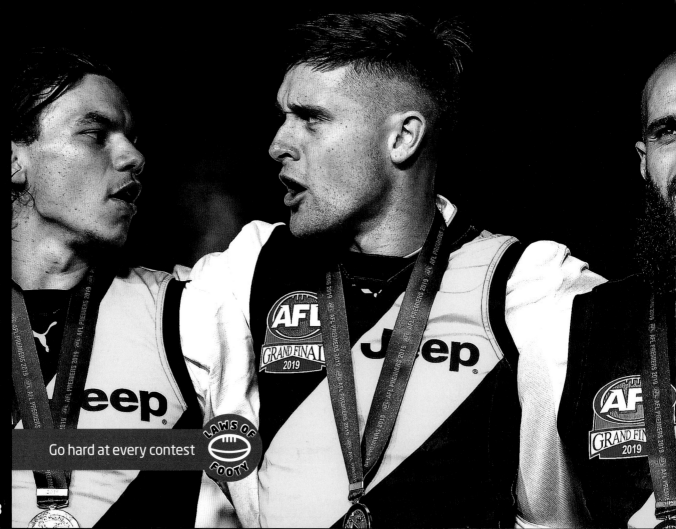

Go hard at every contest

LAWS OF FOOTY

## DID YOU KNOW?

When Australian Football Hall of Fame Legend Ron Barassi signs his name, he adds 17-4-10. Why? He played or coached in 17 Grand Finals for ten wins! He shares the most Premierships with his coach at Melbourne, Norm Smith. Hawthorn's Michael Tuck has won 7 Premierships—the most as a player.

*Ron Barassi 31*
*17410*

## QUICK ? QUIZ

Only one team has received a gold-plated Premiership Cup.

**WHICH TEAM AND WHAT YEAR?**

**CLUE:** it was the year the AFL celebrated its 100th season.

**WINNERS:** The Tigers celebrated their 12th Premiership on stage on the MCG two hours after the final siren, now a traditional post-Grand Final event. They were cheered on by thousands of fans who had stayed at the ground for the music and the presentation of the winners. Here, Daniel Rioli, Jayden Short, Bachar Houli, David Astbury (holding the Cup) join fans for another rendition of the famous club song.

MY WORD!

# COURAGE

If there is one quality that all footballers are expected to possess in abundance, it is courage. Courage is originally from the Latin word, 'cor', which means heart. Coaches and fans expect their players to show plenty of heart in a match, and sometimes a coach needs to give players some heart—that is, encourage them when they're down. Supporters are constantly being encouraged and heartened by their clubs' performances. Of course, fans usually wear their hearts on their sleeves—they scream, shout, even cry, and generally let their feelings be known. The coach might also have a heart-to-heart talk with a player—a talk that might cover personal issues and feelings. A word connected to courage is 'cordial', which has two meanings. A coach may give a cordial welcome to a recruit—a welcome from the heart—and the players might also refresh themselves with a cordial drink. Such drinks were originally thought to be stimulating for the heart!

## QUICK ? QUIZ

Through the AFL Players' Association, players vote for the most courageous player in the League each year— which they've done since 1991. North Melbourne hero Glenn Archer won the award a record six times in his career, but which GWS GIANTS star won it in 2018?

## DID YOU KNOW?

A human's heart beats, on average, 70 times a minute. A mouse's beats about 700 times a minute and an elephant's about 30 times a minute.

**HARD BALL:** Geelong's Joel Selwood (left) and Adelaide's Rory Sloane are two of the hard nuts of AFL football.

## ALL ABOUT... YOUNGEST & OLDEST

The **YOUNGEST** player to make his debut for an AFL club was Claude Clough, who played for St Kilda in round 1, 1900, when he was just 15 years and 209 days. He went on to play 23 games. Many of us know **Tim Watson (below)**, the Essendon champion and now TV and radio star. Tim was 15 years and 305 days when he played the first of his 307 games for Essendon in round 7, 1977. He is the fourth youngest to make his debut, behind Clough, Collingwood and Fitzroy's Keith Bromage and Collingwood's Albert Collier.

Seven players made their debut when aged 15. The **OLDEST** player ever was Vic Cumberland, who played 176 matches for Melbourne and St Kilda, the last in round 16, 1920, at the age of 43 years and 48 days. The oldest of the recent players—and the closest to breaking Cumberland's record—was Essendon's Dustin Fletcher, who played his last AFL game at the age of 40 years and 23 days in 2015. That game was Fletcher's 400th of a stellar career that brought two premierships, two All Australian jumpers, and a club best and fairest.

### QUICK ? QUIZ

Essendon champion Dick Reynolds won the first of his three Brownlow Medals in 1934, aged 19 years and 91 days.

**HE IS THE ONLY TEENAGER TO WIN THE BROWNLOW?**

True or False?

**STAYING POWER:** Dustin Fletcher was the second oldest footballer in history when he played his last AFL game in 2015, at the age of 40 years and 23 days.

### DID YOU KNOW?

Claude Clough's record as the youngest player on debut (15 years, 209 days, on 5 May 1900) cannot be broken under current AFL rules. A player can't be drafted now unless he has reached the age of 18 or will be 18 by April 30 of the year following the AFL National Draft. To be a rookie, he must be 18 on or before December 31 of the draft year.

Follow instructions to the letter

TIM WATSON
ESSENDON

# WESTERN BULLDOGS

| | |
|---|---|
| **ESTABLISHED** | 1883 |
| **CAPTAIN** | Easton Wood |
| **SENIOR COACH** | Luke Beveridge |

For most people living in the western suburbs of Melbourne, there is only one team—the Western Bulldogs. The Bulldogs joined the League in 1925, making them—along with Hawthorn and the Kangaroos—the youngest of the ten Victorian clubs in the AFL, even though, they were first formed in 1883. In 1997, the Bulldogs changed their name from Footscray, after the suburb in which their ground was located; the players still have F.F.C on the back of their guernseys. The Bulldogs had their moment in the sun in 2016, completing one of the most incredible runs to the Premiership, breaking a 62-year drought. Along with Melbourne, the Bulldogs were instrumental in the growth of women's football, hosting the inaugural exhibition game between the two clubs. In the 2018 season, AFLW Bulldogs finished on top of the ladder and went through to win the Grand Final.

## WOOFER'S MAGIC MOMENTS

**1** It's round 21, 2000, and the Bombers are looking for win 21, to remain unbeaten. Enter the Bulldogs, the party-poopers. Coming off wins against Carlton and Collingwood in the previous two weeks, the Bulldogs, brilliantly coached by Terry Wallace, wreck the Bombers' perfect record with an 11-point win.

**2** The 2016 Preliminary Final against the new kids on the block, GWS GIANTS, was a game for the ages at Spotless Stadium in Sydney. With both teams trading blows and the lead changing constantly, the Bulldogs came out on top by 6 points, putting them into their third Grand Final.

**3** 2016 was truly the year of the Dog. As they had done all year, the Bulldogs played with incredible spirit to win their second flag. At the presentation, Luke Beveridge invited injured captain Bob Murphy to the stage to present him with his Jock McHale medal. Murphy, Beveridge and captain Easton Wood held the Cup aloft as one.

Woofer >

# FROM THE BEGINNING

CLUB FORMED: 1883
JOINED THE AFL/VFL: 1925
PREMIERSHIPS:
**2** - 1954, 2016
AFLW PREMIERSHIPS:
**1** - 2018
GAMES RECORD-HOLDER:
Brad Johnson (364)
GOALS RECORD-HOLDER:
Simon Beasley (575)
JOINED THE AFLW: 2017

# CLUB SONG

(TO THE TUNE OF SONS OF THE SEA AN OLD NAUTICAL SONG)

Sons of the west
Red, white and blue
We come out snarling
Bulldogs through and through
Bulldogs bite and Bulldogs roar we give our very best
But you can't beat the boys of the Bulldog breed
We're the team of the mighty west!

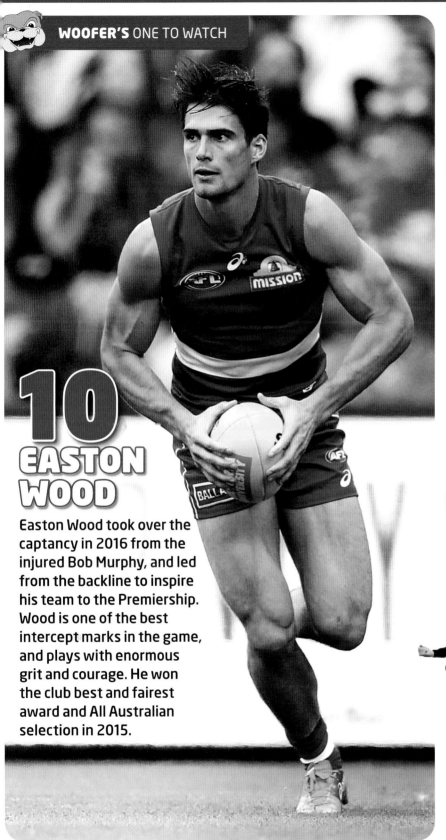

**WOOFER'S** ONE TO WATCH

# 10
# EASTON
# WOOD

Easton Wood took over the captancy in 2016 from the injured Bob Murphy, and led from the backline to inspire his team to the Premiership. Wood is one of the best intercept marks in the game, and plays with enormous grit and courage. He won the club best and fairest award and All Australian selection in 2015.

# QUICK QUIZ

The Bulldogs training ground changed its name from the Western Oval in 1995, to honour the name of its greatest player.

**WHAT IS THE OVAL CALLED?**

**CLUE:** This champion is a Legend of the Australian Football Hall of Fame.

.............................................

**ANSWER**

# DID YOU KNOW?

Since the top eight system of the finals was introduced in 1994, the Bulldogs are the only team to win the Premiership from seventh.

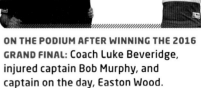

**ON THE PODIUM AFTER WINNING THE 2016 GRAND FINAL:** Coach Luke Beveridge, injured captain Bob Murphy, and captain on the day, Easton Wood.

# WESTERN BULLDOGS .COM.AU

ROXIE'S ONE TO WATCH

## 2
## ELLIE BLACKBURN

Ellie Blackburn has been a star midfielder/forward since making her debut for the Western Bulldogs in round 1 of the 2017 season. She led the team's goalkicking in that first season and was equal best and fairest. She won All Australian honours in her first two seasons and was named in the squad in 2019. In the absence of Katie Brennan, she captained the Bulldogs to win the 2018 flag, and was co-captain in 2019, with Brennan. Her strength, pace and clean hands are lethal at stoppages. Happily for the Bulldogs, she has signed until 2021.

**2019 CAPTAINS**
Ellie Blackburn & Katie Brennan

**2020 SENIOR COACH**
Nathan Burke

One of the 'traditional' clubs of the AFLW, the trailblazing Bulldogs won the Premiership in 2018, the second year of the competition. Any wonder with stars like Ellie Blackburn and Brooke Lochland, the latter of whom kicked a record seven goals against Carlton in 2018.

Roxie >

# COORDINATES

DEGREE OF
DIFFICULTY

★ ★ ☆

This activity is all about following instructions and we all know that the best team players are the ones who listen hard and follow the coach's orders. Follow the directions below to make dots where directed. Join the dots as you make them and see what picture appears on the grid. Start with a fresh dot for each set of different coloured coordinates. You might like to colour the image when you've finished it... especially if you follow the Bulldogs.

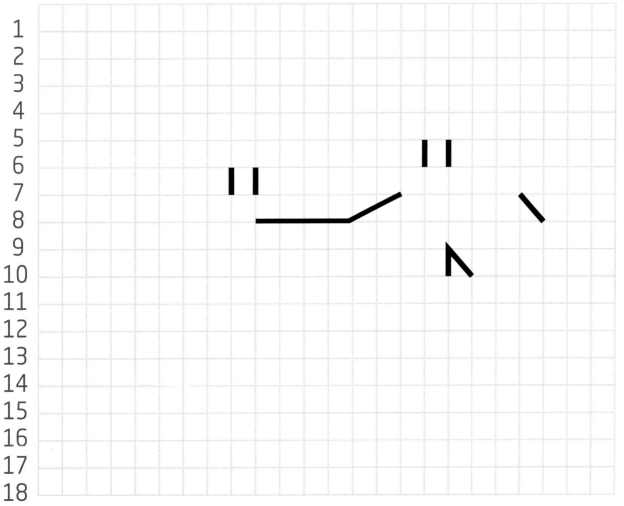

| 1. | D3 | 7. | V2 | 13. | W13 | 19. | A13 | 25. | B5 | 31. | F6 | 37. | F9 | 43. | E10 |
| 2. | E3 | 8. | V3 | 14. | U15 | 20. | E5 | 26. | D3 | 32. | O5 | 38. | L7 | 44. | F11 |
| 3. | F4 | 9. | T3 | 15. | R16 | 21. | D5 | 27. | F6 | 33. | R5 | 39. | P7 | 45. | M11 |
| 4. | K3 | 10. | T4 | 16. | J17 | 22. | D6 | 28. | J6 | 34. | Q6 | 40. | R8 | 46. | R10 |
| 5. | Q3 | 11. | V8 | 17. | C16 | 23. | C7 | 29. | I7 | 35. | M6 | 41. | D9 | 47. | T8 |
| 6. | S1 | 12. | W11 | 18. | A15 | 24. | B6 | 30. | G7 | 36. | O5 | 42. | C10 | | |

# ANSWERS

Page 12: Darcy Vescio.

Page 14: 39 Grand Finals at the MCG. There were 2 in 2010 and the 1991 Grand Final was played at Waverley Park.

Page 15: **JUMP TO IT:** Red jumper $40, blue $30, green $70, gold $80, black $50. Missing totals are $270 (row) and $280 (column).

Page 15: Fremantle needed 11 clean jumpers and the Hawks 5; total=16.

Page 17: Brisbane Bears and West Coast.

Page 18: 4.

Page 19: He needed 51 more goals to make 588, for an average of 6.0 goals per game.

Page 21: 10 goals vs GWS.

Page 23: Rhubarb is often treated like a fruit, but it is a vegetable. All the others are fruit.

Page 24: **Spot 10 Differences**

Page 27: In 1993, Fagan was senior coach of Sandy Bay, in Hobart.

Page 29: **Lucky Locker:** Locker 4.

Page 29: 1959.

Page 30: Tony Lockett.

Page 31: The two 19-year-olds were Daniel Venables (WCE) and Jaidyn Stephenson (Coll.). Stephenson was younger by 57 days.

Page 33: The Silvagni brothers, Jack and Ben. Their grandfather is Sergio, and their father Stephen.

Page 35: **Defence Force**

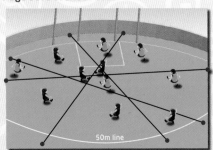

Page 36: Stephen Kernahan captained Carlton in 226 games.

Page 37: 3.

Page 41: North Melbourne.

Page 43: Lance Franklin.

Page 45: Kevin Sheedy.

Page 47: GWS.

Page 48: **Brainbuster**

| Given name | Surname | Item | Price |
|---|---|---|---|
| Jack | Notting | Scarf | $9 |
| Sophie | Johnson | Beanie | $10 |
| Sam | Porter | Flag | $8 |

Page 48: 12:05.

Page 49: One kilogram.

Page 50: MCG.

Page 51: Middle; Goal; Back; Eyes; Trouble.

Page 51: **Talking Footy:** 1. Drop Punt; 2. Game Plan; 3. Goal Post; 4. Team List.

Page 53: 2015.

Page 55: **Footy A to Z**

Page 55: Beep Test.

Page 56: 41 metres.

Page 57: Britannia.

Page 59: Hawthorn.

Page 61: 164 points.

Page 62: 84 points.

Page 63: **Brainbuster**

| First name | Surname | Staff | Position |
|---|---|---|---|
| Jason | Carter | Ms Johnson | Physio |
| Brad | Jones | Ms Derum | Social club manager |
| Shane | Smith | Mr Brown | Football manager |

Page 65: Charlie Dixon.

Page 66: **Perfect Pair:** Images A and B.

Page 67: 43 centimetres.

Page 69: Jeremy Cameron.

Page 71: Malcolm Blight coached North Melbourne, as captain-coach, then Geelong, Adelaide and St Kilda. He won two premierships with Adelaide (1997-98).

Page 72: St Kilda, *When the Saints Go Marching In.*

Page 73: 50.

Page 75: 25.

Page 76: Steve Johnson.

Page 77: They were all captains when they won the Norm Smith Medal.

Page 78: Dustin Martin.

Page 81: Norm Smith.

Page 83: 50.

Page 84: **Spot 10 Differences**

Page 87: Alastair Clarkson (Hawthorn), John Longmire (Sydney) and Adam Simpson (West Coast).

Page 89: Mark Blicavs.

Page 91: Tony Lockett.

Page 93: Warren Tredrea and Jay Schulz.

Page 94: The field umpire calls 'All clear'.

Page 95: **Dripping Wet**

Page 96: **Spot 10 Differences**

Page 99: Essendon and Port Adelaide.

Page 100: Full-back.

Page 101: Sydney and St Kilda.

Page 105: 27.

Page 106: Bernie Quinlan. He shared the 1981 Brownlow Medal with Barry Round.

Page 107: Papua New Guinea.

Page 111: Bob Skilton.

Page 112: 6 goals per game.

Page 113: Bob Pratt (1934).

Page 114: Optus Stadium in Perth.

Pahe 117: Sydney Swans.

Page 119: North Melbourne, 1996.

Page 120: Callan Ward.

Page 121: True. Eight 20-years-old have won the Brownlow.

Page 123: Whitten Oval.

Page 125: **Coordinates**

# AUTOGRAPHS